Not having a father was awkward and inconvenient only for *other* people—never for Brett. In fact, Brett preferred her Mom single. She'd change and be like all the other mothers if she had a husband. Then there'd be three meals on time, a strict bedtime, and probably they'd both have to wear skirts instead of jeans. Life with Mom seemed just right—until the Wolf Man came along.

Brett liked Theo and his wolfhound Norma, but what if he and Mom got married and had babies (even though they promised that didn't have to happen)? Things would change. So Brett, in an attempt to keep her world together, invents a million and one reasons why Mom should stay single. Couldn't the Wolf Man just stay over on weekends? she asks in a feeble attempt to keep the status quo.

Norma Klein has created real and witty—though frequently offbeat—characters in a candid book which speaks to today.

Mom,
The Wolf Man
and Me

Mom,
The Wolf Man
and Me

by Norma Klein

Pantheon

This title list was originally catalogued by the Library of
congress as follows: Klein, Norma, 1938–   Mom, the Wolf
Man, and me. (New York) Pantheon Books (1972)
x, 128 pp 22 cm Summary: An eleven year old girl
describes her life and relationship with her mother who has
never married. (1. Illegitimacy–Fiction. 2. Unwed
mothers I Title. PZ7.K678345 Mo 72-260

ISBN 0-394-82470-9 ISBN 0-394-92470-3 (lib. bdg.)

Manufactured in the United States of America

To my parents

Contents

Mom,
The Wolf Man
and Me

Chapter One

Father's Day

"Where's your father? Did he have to go to work or something?"

It was Father's Day at school and Mary Jane Wakowski was eyeing me with this funny expression. Her father, a sort of fat man with glasses, was off in the corner talking to Mrs. Darling. I gave her a kind of steady, blank look and just said, "No."

"So, where is he?"

"I don't have a father." You've got to say this just the right way and, in fact, I was out of practice, because for years I'd always gone to the same school and everybody knew and didn't ask. I don't really mind if they do, but if they haven't for a long time, you tend not to think of good, quick answers. Evelyn, this girl who lives in my building, says it's the same with her birthmark. She has a birthmark on her leg, a brown spot, and she says there are months and months when practically everyone she meets says, "What's that *thing* on your leg?" or "Did you fall and hit yourself?" (Once she said some little boy asked, "Did a dog go against your leg?") So she has to think of something to say that will sort of put the person in his place or make him feel a little dumb for asking. But then, she says, there are months when nobody asks about it and she forgets it's there. Then, when somebody mentions it again, she's forgotten all her good remarks. That's the way it is with me.

Mary Jane's got a wise expression. She thinks she's very smart because her father, who's a teacher, is always teaching her things at home like algebra so she knows them before anyone at school. "Oh, your parents are divorced, I guess," she said.

"Nope," I said.

Her eyes got bigger. "What do you mean? What are they, then?"

"They aren't divorced," I said. "They were never married."

Some days I kind of like going through this routine, even though it might be easier to say,

4

"They're divorced," since it wouldn't really matter. But I like seeing that expression on people's faces—*sometimes* I like it.

"They have to have been married," she said, almost mad. "You couldn't have been born otherwise."

I smiled.

"Everybody has a mother and a father," she went on. "That's how people get born."

"Is it?" I said.

"A mommy can't do it all by herself," Mary Jane said. "She can't sit on an egg or something."

"Gee, can't she?" I said, looking as bland as vanilla pudding, I hoped.

"You *know* she can't," said Mary Jane, ruffled.

"All I said was, they didn't get married," I said. "I didn't say she sat on an *egg*."

Maybe the light was beginning to dawn in Mary Jane's head, but she still kept looking at me in this funny, puzzled way. Finally, she said, "I never heard of anything like *that*."

Mary Jane is the type who if she never heard of it, thinks it should never have happened. "Live and learn," I said and walked over to the corner to play.

That's the trouble with starting in a new school. The reason I did was that we moved to a different part of New York, and we were in a different district. I was sorry we moved anyway. We used to live in the Village on this little street with trees, where it was quiet most of the time. But Mom said they were going to raise our rent, and she heard of an apartment in a new building uptown right near "a very good school." I guess the school is good, but I don't like the apartment building. It's *too* new. The doorman asks everyone who comes up who they are and that makes a lot of people nervous. He even asks people who've been there before. Mom doesn't like that either. She's always telling him just to let people up if they want to visit us, but he always says, "That's my job, Mrs. Levin."

Mom doesn't mind being called Mrs. Levin, even if she's not married. She says it's a convenience. I guess she doesn't like explaining all the time either. But the people at work call her Miss Levin. When they call up, they ask for her by that name or sometimes just by her first name, Deborah. She's a photographer for a magazine. She takes pictures, mostly of actors and actresses, sometimes of criminals and people along the street and things like that. When I was a baby, and even now, she took hundreds of pictures of me. If I'm just sitting there reading, I'll look up and there's Mom, sneaking up on me with her camera. Sometimes she lets me look through it, and she said that for my next birthday, when I'm twelve, she'll let me have my own camera. Then she says we can go to Africa together and take pictures of wild animals. That's something Mom has always wanted to do and I'd like to do it, too, since I love animals.

The only part that I really mind about Mom not being married is when people ask questions. Otherwise we have a good time, better in some ways than lots of my friends who have mothers *and* fathers. Like, when I visit Andrew, who was my best friend from my old school, everything has to be done at just a certain time. First we have to do our homework, then we can play, and at just a certain time, we have to have dinner. "Don't you see what time it is?" Andrew's mother keeps saying. In our house we hardly even have clocks. Mom never cares what time it is or when we eat. She says I have to go to bed more or less on time but if I don't, she doesn't really care. Maybe it's because her schedule is so odd. She works at night lots of times, developing pictures in our little back room. Sometimes she works all night and then just leaves me breakfast. I eat it by myself and go off to school by myself, too. Sometimes—which seems funny to some people—she's just getting up when I come home from school. Once she was just having breakfast when Andrew and I came in. "How come your mother is in her pajamas?" he said. "Is she sick?"

I felt funny then. I guess I wanted her to be like

Andrew's mother, who is always dressed up and greets us at the door with sandwiches or cookies. So I said she was sick and when Andrew went home, I told Mom she shouldn't just be in pajamas at three in the afternoon. The good thing about Mom is that you can tell her these things. She never gets mad, but she doesn't always do them either. But after that, she tried sleeping in her blue jeans and shirt so that, even if she was just getting up, my friends wouldn't know. I thought that was okay, even though not that many mothers wear blue jeans either. But Mom is just sort of like that. She wears her hair in a pony tail, too, and she never gets dressed up like Evelyn's mother and never puts on makeup. Evelyn and I sometimes watch her mother get dressed up for dates and it takes her hours. She sits in front of this big mirror, that makes her face look gigantic, like a pumpkin. Then she puts on all sorts of stuff and lets us try some, too—moon drops and blushers and eye makeup and perfume. Mom never uses that stuff. If she goes out, she just washes her hair and maybe puts on something different, but not that different from what she was wearing already. She's just that way. Even Andrew says mothers are just a certain way, whatever that way is, and it's silly to think they will ever change. But on the whole, I like Mom the way she is and don't especially mind not having a father.

Andrew's father, for instance, isn't nice at all. He never wants to play with him and he's always telling Andrew he isn't good at things. So mainly he makes Andrew feel worse than he would if he never had a father. There are lots of fathers like that, so I'd rather have none than one of those. Of course, it would be nice to have a great one. Sometimes I pretend Wally, this man that Mom works with, is my real father. (I know he isn't, because Mom said my real father lives in some other city and doesn't even know he's my real father, or that I was even born.) Wally has a wife, actually, but he doesn't like her. Mom says she doesn't like her either. But even though I like Wally, I don't know if I'd want him for a father all the time. He has a funny face, which is one thing I like—it's very round, like a moon, with a long dark moustache that he always pulls on when he's thinking. He always says to me, "Hi, kid. What's new?" He never calls me by my real name, Brett. What I like best is that sometimes, as a special treat, he brings over his movie projector and on Sunday nights, which is the time he has his children visit him, (he has Nicky who is two years younger than me and Marshall who's just three) he shows us all movies and we have pizza sent up and it's a lot of fun. If he lived with us, though, we'd do that every week, and it might not be so much fun. Also, I couldn't do as many things with Mom the way I do now. Most mothers and fathers go off together and leave their children with a babysitter, but Mom lets me come along if I want. If I had a father, maybe she wouldn't.

It's funny. Evelyn, whose parents are divorced, really wants a father. Her mother spends practically all her time going out on dates. Once Evelyn said to me, "That's her work."

"Going out on dates isn't work," I said.

"It *is*," said Evelyn. "She does it to find a father. She doesn't even like it, but she knows she has to."

"Why does she have to?" I said. "Mine doesn't."

"She has to. She goes to look them all over. If she finds a good one, she'll pick him."

There must be a lot of bad ones, because Evelyn's mother has been going on dates for years. Whenever Evelyn and I play, she usually thinks of some game about fathers. Or she'll say, "Wouldn't it be great to have Pat as a father?"

Pat is one of the doormen in our building and he's always joking and telling Evelyn that her uncle's dog, Miffy, this poodle, is in a wooden box that is in the lobby. "I've got him in there. Should I let him out?" He always says that and I don't think it's so funny anymore, but Evelyn really likes him. He always gives Miffy a biscuit, but he makes her dance around on her hind legs, even though she's quite old. Evelyn says Miffy likes that, but I think it's cruel.

"What would be so good about having a father who was a doorman?" I'd say.

"Oh, you'd see him all the time," Evelyn said. "If you came home from school, he'd be right there. And you could play in the lobby if you wanted."

"I guess so."

Personally I can think of things I'd rather do than play in the lobby of our building all afternoon, but Evelyn is like that. She'd give almost anything to have a father. Whenever we go places where you can make a wish, you know she's always wishing about that. Once I even used my wish to wish it for her, but later, when it didn't happen, I was sorry that I threw the wish away. I don't think it ever works if you use your wish up on someone else.

The day they had Father's Day at school, not all of the fathers came. Melinda's mother is divorced and so is Kenneth's, and some of the fathers work, so I didn't feel funny about it. I just don't feel funny about being the only one not to do things. I guess it's my personality. People like my teacher at my old school think I'm pretending about that. I can tell that sometimes they feel sorry for me and they even say I'm being "brave," even if the thing has nothing to do with being brave. It's funny. But, even if all the fathers had come on Father's Day, I wouldn't have minded so much. It's just that they all didn't. But when I came home from school and was having a snack with Mom, I could see she was worried about it.

"Oh, there weren't so many fathers," I said. I even made it seem like there were hardly any so she wouldn't worry about it.

"I could've had Wally come," she said. "He had today off."

"Mom, it didn't matter," I said. "Anyway, Wally's not my father and so it's silly to make things up."

Mom sort of sighed and cut another brownie. "I just hate these rituals!" she said. "All these holidays!"

"I don't," I said. "Some of them are nice."

"It's such a waste of time," she said.

"It's funny," I said. "They don't have a *Mother's* Day at school."

Mom frowned. "Ya, Scratcher, that is funny. Why don't they? . . . I guess it's because some mothers are at the school all the time. They have nothing better to do."

"I guess that's it," I said. I wish Mom wouldn't worry so much about this stuff, but she's that way. Unlike me, she really cares if she's the only one doing something a certain way. And the trouble is, usually she *is* the only one. That's the funny part.

Chapter Two

The Wizard of Oz

"I hear you had Father's Day at school Friday," Wally said. "Why didn't you tell me, kid? I would've liked to come."

I shrugged. "There was nothing to do, really."

"I would've liked it," he said. "I like that sort of thing."

He was setting up the movie, which this night was going to be "The Wizard of Oz." Marshall was fiddling with something on the floor. "Hey, Marshall, come on, cut it out, will you?" Wally said. He never raises his voice or says anything really loud, so his children never listen to him. Especially Marshall, who doesn't seem to listen much anyway. Wally bent down. "It seems like Marshall has been three years old now for about eight years, doesn't it?" he said. "Hey, Marshall, when's your birthday?"

"In a couple of months," Nicky said. He was lying on the floor, reading a comic.

"See, that's what they keep telling me," Wally said. "It's been a couple of months now for, like, eight years."

Mom looked in. "Thayer, what is this? What's taking so long?" She always calls Wally by his last name and he always calls her by her last name.

"You going some place, Levin? You have a date or something?" he said.

"No, but it's . . . what is it . . . oh, forget it." She went back into the darkroom. Mom usually likes to watch the movies with us, but this time she was developing something.

"Have you ever noticed?" Wally said, "how women have this obsession with time? What if all the clocks in the world were destroyed? Life would go on just the same—better probably."

"Usually she's not like that," I said. I was watching Nicky to see what page he was up to. He'd said I could borrow the comic when he was done.

The phone rang, so I answered it. It was Evelyn. "Can I come and watch the movies too?" she said.

Unfortunately, I had told Evelyn we were seeing "The Wizard of Oz," which happens to be one of her favorites. She always imagines that the Tin Man is her father. Personally I think he'd make a lousy father, but as I've said, Evelyn is like that. "I thought your mother was out," I said.

"Ya, well, the babysitter doesn't mind. She can watch T.V."

"She can watch the movie, too," I said.

"Gee, could she? You wouldn't mind?"

I put my hand over the phone. "Wally, can Evelyn and her babysitter watch the movie, too?"

Wally said, "Evelyn and her babysitter and even her babysitter's babysitter can watch the movie."

"Sure," I told Evelyn.

Evelyn's babysitter turned out to be quite nice, not like that old Mrs. Wizen, who Evelyn's mother usually gets. We both hate Mrs. Wizen. She always eats these disgusting health foods that make her breath smell—sauerkraut juice and little ground wheat things that she says are good for her "bowels." But this babysitter was sort of young, a college girl, I guess. She had a long pigtail down her back. That's the way I'd like to wear my hair, but it's never gotten long enough.

"Hello, babysitter," Wally said.

"Her name is Marilyn Anne Richardson," said Evelyn.

"Hello Marilyn Anne Richardson, then," Wally said. "Okay, is everybody ready? I think I'm about set."

"I think I'll sit over here," Evelyn said.

There is one funny thing about Evelyn: she wears glasses, but she's ashamed about it. For a while she tried wearing contact lenses but they kept popping out at the wrong times. Once Evelyn and I spent almost an hour looking for one of her contact lenses on Fifth Avenue when we were waiting for a bus. A whole crowd came to help us look after a while. I can't understand why Evelyn is so vain, but maybe I would be, too, if I were extremely pretty. Everyone says Evelyn is extremely pretty. She has this very neat face with very small features and the kind of hair that's very black and flat next to her head. My face is okay, but compared to her all my features are very big, and my hair is the kind that always flops all over the place, whether it's short or long. Even Mom says I'm not beautiful. She even gets mad if Grandma says I am. She says I'm just in-between, which is the best—not so ugly that no one will want to look at me and not so pretty that it will make a mess of my life. I don't see exactly why being pretty should make a mess of my life. Except once, when I was visiting Evelyn this man came in, some date of her mother's, and after we'd been talking

16

to him for a while, he said to Evelyn, "You're a very beautiful girl. Some day you'll have the power to make men very unhappy. I hope you won't." He didn't say anything to me, so I guess I won't have the power to make anybody unhappy. In fact, he didn't even seem to notice me that much, which I didn't mind since he didn't seem very nice. Pat, the doorman, sometimes calls me Snow White, because my hair is blond (but it's really dirty blond) and Evelyn Rose Red, because hers is black. "There come my two fairy princesses," he'll say. But in school I'm never the one picked for fairy princesses, more likely the dog or cat or something. Anyway, it seemed funny to me that even now with just us—Wally and Nicky and her babysitter—Evelyn should be too vain to wear her glasses. I knew if her mother was there, she'd make her wear them, but I didn't say anything.

The movie was good. Marshall got a little scared at the part about the Wicked Witch of the East and that made Nicky laugh, because he likes the Wicked Witch best. "That Good Witch is ugly, ugh," he said in the middle, when we were having popcorn and Wally was changing reels. "She's so old!"

"Witches *have* to be old," Evelyn said. "That's how they learn all their magic."

"She's not a *real* witch, anyway," I said, reaching for the popcorn. "She's just an actress playing a witch."

"Don't be a spoilsport, kid," Wally said.

"She is," I said. "You don't think she's a real witch, do you?"

"When I'm watching it, I like to think she's a real witch," Wally said. "Otherwise it wouldn't be as much fun."

"But way *way* back in your mind, you know she's not," I said. "Don't you?"

"Sure, I guess."

Evelyn said, "You never want to think of imaginary things. I love imaginary things . . . Anyway, some of those things might really be true . . . we just don't know for sure."

"We *do* know," I said. Evelyn and I argue about this lots of times, especially when we're dressing up in costumes and she almost gets to believe that she really is whatever she's dressed up like.

At that point Mom looked in and said, "Wallace, it's your dear wife on the phone." She only calls Wally "Wallace" at certain times.

"How come your mother always wears blue jeans?" Nicky said to me when she and Wally had both gone into the other room.

"She says it's more comfortable."

"But she doesn't look like a mother, then," he said.

"She does to me."

"My mother says she would only wear blue jeans on weekends," Evelyn put in, "in the country."

"Well, we never go to the country," I said.

"My mother is too fat to wear blue jeans," Nicky said. "She'd bust right out of them." He laughed.

"She'll never get a new husband if she's so fat," Evelyn said. Evelyn has a one track mind about that, as I've mentioned.

"She doesn't want one," Nicky said. "Why should she?"

"To keep her company," Evelyn said.

Nicky stood on his head. He can do this very fast because he's as thin as a rail. He can turn good cartwheels too. "She has me," he said.

"You're not company," Evelyn said. "You're just a child."

"Know what Mom says about Dad?" Nicky said. He was still on his head so it was hard to look at him. It made you sort of dizzy. "She says he's a baby."

Evelyn frowned. "How can he be a baby?"

Nicky smiled an upside down smile. Wally came back in the room. Nicky jumped back right side up. "Hi, baby," he said to Wally.

Wally looked puzzled. "Hi, baby to you," he said. Wally never minds what you call him.

"On with the show!" said Nicky. He gave Marshall a shove. "Down in front!" he said. Nicky wants to make his own movies. He says I can have a part, if I want, but I said I'd rather help him make them. He said maybe I could, but I have to learn a lot of things first. Nicky is smart for his age in some things, but not at school. He's been to five schools and he never likes them. He never does his work and the teachers are always mad at him. He doesn't care, though.

We watched the rest of "The Wizard" and even Mom came in for the part where the Wicked Witch melts into a pool of water. That was the only part Marshall seemed to like, for some reason. He laughed so much Nicky had to sit on him to keep him quiet.

Chapter Three

Mr. Jones
and the Alligator

Thursdays, after school, I go to Grandma and Grandpa's house. Grandma and Grandpa never lock their door. They must be the only people in New York City that don't, but they have never been robbed or anything. Partly it's because Grandpa is a doctor with his own office right in their living room and his patients have to come in and out. Grandpa is a psychoanalyst. People come and lie down on his couch and tell him their problems. He sits in a black chair next to the table with a big box of tissues on it. If they get very sad and cry, he gives them a tissue. Sometimes when I visit Grandpa, we pretend he's the patient and he lies down on the couch and I sit in his chair. Sometimes he pretends to cry when he makes up his problems which are usually silly, like that he has an alligator in his bathtub and can't take a bath.

Then I hand him a kleenex and say, "Don't cry, Mr. Jones."

He says, "I must, I must." And he makes loud, snuffling sounds. "I love my alligator," he'll say. "What shall I do, Doctor?"

"You must build him a cage," I'll say, "someplace where he'll have lots of room to crawl around. The bathtub is too small for him."

"That's what I keep telling him," Grandpa says, "but he won't listen to me . . . Doctor, it's been six weeks since I took a bath. No one will come near me!"

"You do smell a little funny, Mr. Jones," I said.

"I know," Grandpa says sadly. "I even tried to take a bath with my alligator, but he said it was too crowded . . . He wouldn't even let me share the washcloth with him."

"You do have a problem, Mr. Jones," I say, trying not to laugh. "Well, I see our time is up. Goodbye, Mr. Jones."

"Goodbye, Doctor," Grandpa says. "I feel much better, just from talking to you."

"Good luck, Mr. Jones," I say.

"Thank you, Doctor."

"Give my best to your alligator."

"I'll do that, Doctor . . . He sends his best to you, too." Then Grandpa gets up and pretends to walk out, except sometimes he bumps into Grandma, who is just coming in to see what we're up to or to say dinner is ready. Grandpa only has one thing for dinner: steak, except when he goes to the Chinese restaurant. He also likes caviar. He calls bread, butter and caviar: b, b, and c. I like it too. I like it when the caviar eggs sort of burst in your mouth with a nice salty taste. What I drink at Grandma and Grandpa's house is grape juice. Grandpa drinks coffee out of a big mug (which is really a flowerpot) and Grandma is always having a cup of tea.

But today things were different at Grandma and Grandpa's house, because Grandpa was going to the hospital for an operation tomorrow. Mom said Grandpa was scared and that's why he acted so jolly. I said Grandpa always acted that way, but she said now he was more that way. He even seemed too tired to play our Doctor game, though he was lying on his couch when I came in.

"How is your alligator today, Mr. Jones?" I said, settling into the chair.

Grandpa sighed. "Not too well, I'm afraid, Doctor."

"Oh, is he sick, Mr. Jones?" I said.

"Very sick," Grandpa said.

"Is it a special alligator sickness?" I said.

"Yes, it is," Grandpa said. "My alligator is so sick, he's afraid he will die."

Suddenly I had a funny feeling in my stomach. I wondered if Grandpa was afraid he was going to die. Mom had said his operation was "major" but that people usually lived after it. I said, "No, he won't die, Mr. Jones. I spoke to his doctor. He said things will be fine . . . What your alligator needs is . . . some b, b, and c!"

"Do you think that will cure him?"

"I do, Mr. Jones," I said. "That's just what alligators need when they're sick."

"Maybe you're right, Doctor," Grandpa said. He sat up.

Together we walked into the kitchen. Grandpa keeps all his caviar in a box under the kitchen table. There must be a hundred jars of caviar there. While he was taking one out, Grandma walked in and said, "So, you saw "The Wizard of Oz" again on Sunday?"

I nodded.

"Now, isn't that amazing, that situation with Wally?" she said. She was looking at Grandpa, but he didn't say anything so I asked,

"What's so amazing?"

I happen to know Grandma would like Mom to

marry Wally. She thinks he's in love with Mom, even though Mom says they're just friends. I really think that Grandma would like Mom to be married to someone. In that way, she's like Evelyn. She never says that's what she thinks, but I can tell it is. Grandpa is more like me. He doesn't really care. When he's in the car with Grandma and Mom and me, he always says, "Now look at these three splendid girls. Who has three more splendid girls than these, will you tell me that?" Grandpa is like Pat, the doorman, in that he likes to joke around and says the same things over and over again.

"He's had such problems with those children," Grandma said.

"Nicky?" I said.

"Nicky is the least of it," Grandma said.

"Brett," said Grandpa, "you know what your Grandma needs?"

"What?"

"A little b, b, and c, of course," Grandpa said.

Grandma doesn't like b, b, and c. She likes toasted English muffins, but Grandpa always says that anyway. When Grandma said, "No thanks," Grandpa said, "No b, b, and c? How can that be? Doctor, what is wrong with this fine woman?"

"Mr. Jones," I said, "that fine woman . . . is allergic to b, b, and c."

"Allergic?" said Grandpa. "How can that be?"

"Do you know what happens if she eats even a spoonful?" I said.

"No, what happens?"

"She turns bright purple . . . and her hair turns bright green."

"Sounds very colorful," Grandpa said. "I'd like to see that happen."

"No, you wouldn't," I said, "because when that happens, anyone who looks at her is blinded!"

"Wow!" said Grandpa. "Keep that caviar away from that lady! Don't let her have a speck."

"I won't."

"Even if she begs on her hands and knees, don't let her taste so much as a tiny, tiny mouthful."

"Joe," said Grandma. I could tell she thought we were being silly.

"Yes, Mrs. Jones," Grandpa said.

By the way, Grandpa and Grandma's real name is Levin, just like Mom's.

"Oh, I forget what I was going to say," Grandma said. "What is wrong with me?"

"You're getting old, Mrs. Jones," Grandpa said.

Grandma didn't say anything. I said, "Where's my b, b, and c, Mr. Jones?"

"Coming up, coming up," Grandpa said.

That night Mom said, "How did Grandpa seem?"

"He seemed sad in the beginning," I said. I looked at Mom, who also looked sad. "Will he die, do you think?"

Mom's face didn't change so much but she said, "He's not supposed to."

That night I began thinking that just at certain times I would like to have a father. Someone a little bit like Grandpa, a little bit like Wally, but different. The funny thing is that I can't imagine Mom with a husband. I don't know why that is. I mean, I can imagine me with a father but not her with a husband. I guess because for me to have a father, I wouldn't have to be any different. But for her to have a husband, I guess I imagine she would have to stop wearing blue jeans and having her hair in a pony tail and have to do more regular things. The other thing is that I don't think Mom would want a husband. I mean, I'm certainly not like Evelyn, because most of the time I really don't mind having no father. I really mean that. But sometimes, like tonight, I do mind somewhat, and I wonder if Mom ever has those times. Even though we talk about lots of things and she always says she would tell me anything I wanted to know, we never talk about this. I guess partly it's that I never ask her, and partly because I don't want her to think I'm nudging her or that she should marry just anyone.

I feel worried about Grandpa.

Chapter Four

Mom and Grandma Have an Argument

The weekend Grandpa was going to have his operation, Mom had to go away on an assignment. She was going to Chicago to take pictures for a trial there. Grandma was sort of mad that Mom was going. The reason I know this is that on Friday afternoon Grandma came over with some cookies. They were the kind of cookies I like best, that sort of crunchy kind with pieces of candied fruit and chocolate in them. I had some homework which I wanted to get finished, because I was going to Evelyn's for the weekend. The reason I wasn't going to Grandma's is that she was going to be busy seeing how Grandpa was and things like that. Anyway, in some ways I think Mom likes it better when I go to Evelyn's, even though she's not that crazy about Evelyn's mother. I like to go to Evelyn's, too, since, except for her thing about wanting a father, she can be a lot of fun. So I wanted to get my homework done—then we could spend the whole time playing and stuff. So I took a bunch of cookies in my room and sat on the floor doing the math we had for Monday. But while I was doing it, I could hear Grandma and Mom arguing. I didn't really listen, because I kind of knew what it was about anyway. But on the other hand, I'm quite good at math and don't have to concentrate that hard when I do it, so I couldn't help partly listening to them just to keep from being bored. Mom always says she can't understand my being good at math, since she always hated it, but she says maybe now they do it in a new way that is better. Mom even counts on her fingers sometimes; it's odd.

Grandma was mad because she didn't think Mom should be going away when Grandpa was going to have his operation.

"Oh, Mother," Mom was saying, "you know I can't see him for five days, anyway, if he's in Intensive Care."

"What if something happens?" Grandma said.

"If something happens, you'll call me and I'll come right home. You have my number."

Then there was a pause, probably Grandma sighing, and then Grandma said, "I just don't know, Deborah . . . all this obsession with career . . ."

Mom was getting mad, as she often does when she talks to Grandma. "If it weren't for my work, I'd die!"

"That's just what I mean," Grandma said.

This went on for a while. It's funny. I guess the reason Mom doesn't get along with Grandma is that Mom is an extremist. That means someone who says things very loudly in a way that seems mad. I never do that. Even when I'm mad, I guess I tend not to say anything. Mom thinks that's terrible. She said when I was a baby, she was always telling me to break things and knock things down, but I never did. I always just sat there. So I guess I was just born that way. Like I never have fights with Grandma. I almost never have fights with Mom, either. Maybe if I had a brother or a sister, I'd fight with them, the way Andrew does with Colette, his baby sister, who's always knocking things down. But not having ever had one, I don't know.

I listened to them arguing for a while, but it wasn't that interesting. There was just one part when Grandma said, "What can *she* think when you behave this way?"

I can tell when she means me because of how Grandma says it.

"I wish to hell *you* were more like *her!*" Mom says. "Brett understands me better than anyone. She's the best person around here!"

That made me feel good in a way. The best thing about Mom is that she never says what she doesn't mean. Grandma thinks she should—they've had arguments about that, too. But I know Mom really does feel that way about me. When I was little—this is one of the few things I remember from when I was really little, like four or five— Mom and I used to play this game, where I would be the Mommy and she would be the baby. I would get her ready for bed, tuck her in, read her a story, and sometimes at the end, she would say, "I wish you *were* my Mommy" in a way that made me think she really did. I don't mind that.

I had finished my homework, so I went back into the kitchen.

"Grandpa's going to be all right," I said to Grandma who was just sitting there looking mad and sad and sort of fiddling with the tea bag out of her tea cup.

"Of course he is!" Mom said.

"I don't think he wants everyone to sit around worrying about him," I said.

"Of course he doesn't," Mom said.

"Well, yes." Grandma pushed out her lips in

this way she has, sort of a bad habit. "No, I'm not worried. Did I tell you, I met his doctor? Such a charming man, an Italian with a lovely name, what was it? Was it Primavera? Bonaventura? Something just lovely. I just adore Italians."

"I don't," Mom said.

"Well, this doctor was one of the loveliest men I've ever met," Grandma said and she jumped up.

"I'm sure he's a very fine doctor," Mom said.

Then Grandma left. After she did Mom said, "Whew!" and made supper for us. On Fridays we usually have tartar steak, which started when I was a baby and used to like raw hamburger better than cooked. Mom likes it raw, too. We put stuff on it like capers and Mom puts a raw egg on hers, the yolk part, (but to me that looks too slimy), and catsup and really whatever we like. We both think that's one of the best things to eat but I've found most people, even Wally, think it's disgusting.

"Do you think Mothers are a good idea?" Mom said.

"What do you mean?" I said.

"Maybe children should be brought up separately, just with other children."

"But that would be noisy," I pointed out. "And you probably wouldn't have your own room."

"Ya, that's true," Mom said.

Then she packed her stuff in her old duffle bag while I lay on her bed and watched.

"I wish I could go to this trial," I said. "I never was at one."

"I know darling," Mom said. "I wish you could, but they just don't allow children under sixteen in the court room, that's all. In a few weeks we can go on that march in Washington, though."

"Is Wally going to that?" I said.

"I don't know, maybe. Why?"

"Just wondered."

"Wally is sweet, isn't he?" Mom said.

"Nicky is sort of funny," I said, laughing. I remembered how he stood on his head all of a sudden.

"Mom..."

"Ya?"

"Do you really think Grandpa will be all right?"

Mom sighed. "Scratcher, I said I did, and I do. But, you know, everybody worries about these things . . . I worry too . . . But you just have to do other things and not think about it and soon it will be over; then you'll be visiting him and your worries will seem far away."

"But you said I can't visit him in the hospital," I pointed out.

"He'll be home, though," Mom said, "Anyhow,

you can speak to him on the phone . . . He'd love that. It would cheer him up more than anything."

"It's funny," I said, putting a pillow on my head. "Evelyn doesn't even have a grandpa or even an aunt or cousins . . . Just one uncle."

"Yelp! Speaking of Evelyn," Mom said.

"I'll go myself," I said. "I have my stuff packed."

Chapter Five

A Weekend
at Evelyn's

Evelyn lives on the other side of the building, so I had to go down in our elevator, then across the lobby, then up in her elevator. Once, Evelyn and I had this idea that when Mom went away, we could just stay by ourselves in my apartment and pretend it belonged just to us. The only trouble would be at night, when Evelyn's mother would want us to have a babysitter. But in a few years we'll be old enough to *be* babysitters, so I don't see how it would matter that much.

Evelyn's mother was going out on a date, as usual. She was in her bedroom doing her hair. Evelyn's mother is one of these people who always looks nice. Even in the morning, when she comes out to make breakfast, she wears this robe with flowers and has her hair brushed. Sort of the opposite of people in my family. I once asked Evelyn if her mother ever looked bad, like when she was sick, and she said no. Even when her mother is sick, she said, she puts on all her makeup and fixes her hair. She says it makes her feel better. Mom thinks that's crazy. That's one thing she doesn't like about Evelyn's mother and I guess Evelyn's mother thinks Mom is sort of a slob, which is true in a way. Once Evelyn's mother was at our house and dropped a pen, she pulled out the bureau to get it. Behind the bureau was all this dust and old pencils and junk and she just sort of gasped as though she'd seen a dead body and Mom started laughing and Evelyn's mother got mad.

Evelyn's mother feels sorry for me, because she thinks Mom doesn't take care of me in the right way. Evelyn told me that. Like this time, when I came in, she said, "Oh, Brett, we're so glad you can be with us. I feel so terrible about your poor grandfather. At his age! You must be so worried."

I don't know why, but there are times when Evelyn's mother makes you feel worse by being nice.

"Mom, can I put on some of that perfume?" Evelyn said.

"No, darling, that was a special gift and it's very expensive. You put on that other one in the green bottle."

Evelyn's mother has a whole room just for putting on her makeup. It has lots of mirrors so you can see yourself from all angles. In some ways it's a little scary, because all kinds of bad things that you might not have noticed can be seen very clearly. It's almost like our science lab at school—there are so many bottles and jars and brushes. You'd think Evelyn's mother was really very ugly, since she spends so much time putting on all this stuff but, in fact, she's very pretty—just like Evelyn.

Evelyn squirted some perfume on me, though I've told her I don't like it. It's so strong it makes me feel funny. "Yuk!" I yelled and leaped back and ran into Evelyn's room.

Unlike me, Evelyn is very neat. Grandma would like her because she only plays with one thing at a time. She has a four-poster-bed with white ruffles and a huge Raggedy Ann doll that is almost as big as Evelyn, and a bright orange rug which is wooly, like a sheep. I looked to see if Evelyn had any new books. She gets mad at me for reading at her house, but her uncle is a publisher and she gets all these free books, so it's better than going to the library.

"Who's her date with?" I said.

"John," Evelyn said.

"Do you like him?"

Evelyn wrinkled her nose. "He's shorter than her."

"So?"

"He has this worried look and he's always sniffing—I think he has asthma. You'll see."

When Evelyn was little, she actually used to train herself to wake up when her mother came home from a date, and she would come out in her pajamas. Her mother got mad at that, but she made her mother promise that she could always come out and meet who she was going out with. Mom doesn't think that's so nice of Evelyn, but it is sort of interesting. Some of the men try to make Evelyn like them—some even bring presents—but once one of them just sat there, reading his newspaper like he didn't even notice us. Even when we began making faces and giggling, he didn't look up and, finally, we had to run out of the room.

The door bell rang. Evelyn ran to answer it. "Hi, John," she said.

I thought John seemed fairly nice, but Evelyn is very strict about who she likes, because she thinks if she says someone is great, her mother might marry that person just to please her. At least I know Mom wouldn't do that.

John came into the living room and just stood there.

"Mother will be with you in a minute," Evelyn said, staring at him. Sometimes I think she makes the dates uncomfortable by staring that way. She says she can put a hex on them if she doesn't like them so they won't call back. I would never tell anyone this, but Evelyn has done some very mean things. If someone she doesn't like calls, she'll say her mother is getting married to someone else. She always says, "The child has to approve" if the mother is getting married, and she's just doing what this book she got says she has a right to do. The book is called *A Child's Guide to Divorce* and Evelyn thinks it's great. Since my parents aren't divorced, I never read it that much.

After Evelyn's mother left and Mrs. Wizen had come and settled down in front of the "telly" as she calls it, we went in and began trying on costumes. Evelyn has some really beautiful old costumes that her mother got from someone. She says she wants to be an actress, which is what her mother once was. Her mother was a dancer, singer, and actress, and Evelyn has a whole album with pictures of her doing stuff like that. Now she just goes on dates.

"Now imagine this," Evelyn said, putting on a tall black hat. "You're walking down the street in some strange city . . ."

"Washington," I said. "We're going there in a few weeks."

"Okay, Washington . . . You're walking along, whistling casually, when suddenly a man approaches and says, 'You're my daughter, my long, lost daughter.'"

"How would he know?"

This is the sort of game Evelyn thinks is great, the "what if" type of game.

"He could tell by the . . . freckle behind your left ear."

I *do* have a freckle behind my left ear. Evelyn and I once really searched because we thought we might become spies and would need identifying characteristics. "But he never saw me, so he never saw my freckle," I said, giggling.

"Well, he saw you when you were born," she said.

"No," I said. "He never knew I was born."

Evelyn can't understand this, though I've explained it to her before. I used to think she was stupid. "But if your mother got pregnant and everything, he must have known!"

"Why?"

"Because she'd be fat. You know, the way pregnant women are."

"But he never saw her like that." I must admit it's hard to imagine Mom looking fat anyway.

"He must've seen her!" Evelyn said.

"No . . . He didn't even live where she did . . ."

Evelyn said, "She could've written him a letter."

"Ya."

"So, how come she didn't?"

"She didn't feel like it."

"But what if he would've liked it, maybe he would've wanted to marry her."

"I guess she didn't want to marry him."

Evelyn frowned. "Was he horribly ugly or what?"

It's typical of Evelyn that the only reason she can think of for not wanting to marry someone is because they're too ugly. "Maybe he didn't have a nice personality," I said. "He might have been sort of dull or dumb or something."

"But you still should marry someone if you're pregnant," Evelyn said.

"Why?" I said. I took up Evelyn's Raggedy Ann doll and sat it on my knee.

"For the child," Evelyn said. I could tell this was probably something she read in her book called *A Child's Guide to Divorce*.

"What if the child didn't like him either?" I said.

That sort of stumped Evelyn. She lay down on the floor and began wiggling her toes in the air.

Lately she's been mad because this summer her mother doesn't want her to go to Europe to visit her father's parents the way she usually does.

Evelyn says she likes going there, even though her grandma and grandpa don't even know English that well and are quite old. But they always love to see her, she says, and they let her stay up till whenever she wants and never even ask if she's brushed her teeth or anything. "When I'm twenty-one, I'm going to live with my father," she said.

"What if he's married to someone else then?" I said.

"That doesn't matter . . . I could be the baby-sitter. Or we could just travel together and I could be the secretary. There're lots of things I could do."

"Would he like it?" I said.

Evelyn smiled. "Sure! Because by then I'd be very attractive and very charming . . . He could even pretend I was his wife."

Somehow, like all Evelyn's plans, this one seemed a little odd and not that likely to me, but I didn't say anything. Evelyn sat up. "Let's scare Mrs. Wizen!" she said.

"How?" I said.

She smiled mysteriously. "I know how! Come on, do what I do . . ."

I knew Grandpa must be all right. Otherwise, Grandma would have called Evelyn's mother. Still, I kept thinking about it all that weekend. I kept thinking of the alligator, too, and of how lonely he must be all by himself in that bathtub with no one to talk to or take baths with.

Mom came back Sunday night. She came over to Evelyn's house to pick me up. By then I was glad to see her, partly because I was getting tired of Evelyn. This makes me wonder about how married people can stand to see each other *every* day—even if they like each other.

The other trouble was it rained Sunday and there was nothing to do, since we'd played all Evelyn's games already. I wouldn't have minded reading, but Evelyn wanted to do things like look people's names up in the phone book and write them imaginary letters and stuff like that. When Mom finally came in, I was so glad to see her, I ran right over and jumped in her arms. She doesn't mind, but Evelyn's mother looked at us in a funny way. I guess she thinks that's not grown-up. Also, Mom looked a little grubby—she probably hadn't taken a bath since she came back.

"How was the trial?" I said.

"Oh, it was great," Mom said. "You know, you could've come, Scratcher. Next time I'll take you. No one would've noticed."

"Do they let children in the courtroom?" Evelyn's mother said.

Mom shrugged. "I bet you could arrange it. So, how was this wild old thing? Did she give you trouble?"

"Brett's never any trouble," Evelyn's mother said, smiling in that way she has.

"She's not?" Mom pretended to look surprised. She likes to pretend to other people that I'm terribly hard to take care of and very wild.

That night, even though it was Sunday, Wally didn't come over, because it was too late. Mom took a shower and washed her hair and while she was drying it, I came in and we spoke to Grandma on the phone. She said Grandpa was in the Intensive Care ward, but that his operation had gone all right.

Mom looked at me and smiled.

"Scratcher, if I get the way Grandma is, will you shoot me?"

"You are like that to me," I said, smiling.

"What? Help!"

Mom began cutting her toenails. "Was the weekend okay?"

I nodded. I lay back on Mom's bed and put two pillows on my head. "You know, I was thinking this thing . . ." I said to Mom. Actually, it was funny, because till I said it, I hadn't thought I was going to tell Mom at all. It was just something I'd been thinking of.

"What sort of thing?" Mom stopped cutting and looked at me.

I put the pillow up so I could only see part of

her face. "Maybe I'll write a letter to my real father."

Mom didn't say anything. Finally she said, "I don't know his address."

"You know his name, don't you?" I said.

"Ya . . . but why, honey? I mean, it would seem odd, wouldn't it? Would it make sense?"

I swallowed. "No, I guess not . . . Evelyn just thought I should."

"Oh, Evelyn!" Mom's voice sounded normal again.

I laughed. "Evelyn always has these ideas—like that if you've never met your real father, he might turn out to be a prince or someone very rich."

"Ya, sounds very likely . . . Well, on that score I can . . ."

"No, *I* don't think it," I said. "Evelyn does."

"Evelyn's going to have problems when she grows up," Mom said. She scooped up her toenail pieces and threw them in the direction of the wastepaper basket. Most of them fell in.

"She has a very lively imagination," I said. "Her teacher at school says it's the best she ever saw . . . She can make up anything."

"I bet she can."

I could see that telling Mom hadn't made her like Evelyn any more. "I wish *I* had a lively imagination," I said. Really, I don't. I just said it

to change the subject, sort of. That got me thinking of the alligator and Grandpa again. As soon as
he was out of the Intensive Care ward, Mom said
I could speak to him on the phone and we could
do Mr. Jones stuff again.

Chapter Six

Andrew

There's one trouble with my new school and moving—I don't see Andrew that much anymore. Evelyn is okay, and I like her, but Andrew was really my best friend, and at the old school I used to see him every day. Now, since he lives in the Village, it's too hard, since you have to take two subways to get to his house. But that Sunday, since Mom had a job in the Village, she said I could go and have supper there and she would pick me up later.

Andrew is funny, in a way. Remember how I said I sometimes get Evelyn mad by just reading or something when she wants to play or make things up? Well, Andrew is like that, only even more. Sometimes if you visit him, he just reads the whole time and hardly even talks to you. He doesn't even know he's doing it. I mean, he doesn't do it to be mean and usually I read, too. But Andrew's mother doesn't like it. She always wants Andrew to get fresh air so he will get bigger—he's the smallest one in his class. Whenever we went to his house after school, all his mother would ask him was if he'd climbed on the monkey bars after school. She thinks that will make him stronger. Andrew always says yes, though in fact there aren't any monkey bars at the school. And if there were, I'm sure he wouldn't use them anyway.

This Sunday Andrew's father was there, too. He's a rabbi and he stays home on Sunday. On Saturdays he can't do anything, not even take a shower. And Andrew's mother can't do anything either, not even cook. On those days Andrew isn't even allowed to go on the monkey bars, even if he wanted to. It's odd: Grandma, Grandpa and Mom are Jewish, but they never talk about it or do anything about it except make jokes sometimes. But Andrew's family really talks about it all the time. They think it's strange that I don't know anything about it. Andrew thinks it's strange, too, but he doesn't care. That's one good thing about Andrew: he never cares how you are, like if you're in a bad mood or something. Also, he never asks about my father or wants to do imaginary things. The thing he really likes to do is experiment with his chemistry set. Andrew is the only one I know who likes science besides me. Mom doesn't know anything about it and neither does Grandma. Grandpa says he does, but when you ask him to explain something, he gets it all mixed up. But Andrew knows a lot, even more than the teacher at school. Andrew's mother says that when she was pregnant with Colette, Andrew knew more about embryos and stuff than she did. It's seems funny to me that someone could be pregnant and not even know all those things.

"Daddy, Brett is going on that march to Washington next week," Andrew said when we were having supper. (Andrew calls his parents Mommy and Daddy, which to me sounds funny, like he was still a baby.)

"What march is that?" Andrew's mother said. She's a sort of plump woman with grey hair. I guess she doesn't dye it like Grandma does. To me, she looks more like a grandmother than a mother.

"The Peace March," Andrew's father said. I know he doesn't think it's good that Mom goes to march because she did once before, and I heard him say something in Yiddish to Andrew's mother and Andrew said later that it hadn't been that nice.

"They'd be willing to take me," Andrew said.

In a way that's probably true, though I hadn't really asked Mom. The thing is, I sort of knew Andrew's parents would say no.

"Andrew, really, you're so comical," his mother said. She talks in this slow way, with a little bit of an accent—I think it's German. "You couldn't possibly go on an adventure like that at your age."

"Brett's going."

"Brett is probably going with her Grandma and her Grandpa and many other adults . . ."

"No, it's just me and Mom," I said, "and maybe Wally and his kids, except maybe not Marshall."

Andrew's mother sighed. "Abe, please, will you stop eating and say something?"

"Andrew knows he cannot go," Andrew's father said. He always talks in this deep voice, like someone in a play. I always have the feeling that people with beards talk that way.

"Shit," Andrew said. "When I grow up and become a drug addict, you'll be sorry you didn't let me do anything when I was a child."

"Somehow I fail to see the connection between those two statements," Andrew's father said. He always talks that way—as though he thought of the whole sentence ahead of time, with all the periods and commas, and then said it.

"And I don't think I approve of Andrew's choice of certain words at the table," Andrew's mother said.

"Which word didn't you like? Grow?" Andrew said. He likes to tease his mother.

"You know the word," his mother said.

"Anything?" Andrew said.

"Andrew, stop showing off in front of Brett," his father said.

Andrew has this very innocent expression. Really, he hardly ever curses, except in front of his mother. With most people, it's usually the other way around.

"You should hear the words Brett uses!" Andrew said.

"I do not!" I said. He makes that up to get his mother mad at me, too.

"Wow, Brett knows more curses than a stevedore," Andrew said. He likes to use words like that.

"Abe!" Andrew's mother said.

"Ignore him, Sylvia," said Andrew's father. He eats very fast and is always done before everyone else. Then he gets a big glass of tea and sits down in this chair with wings on each side of it and reads the paper. Then Andrew and I can go into his room and play.

"Maybe I'll sneak out and go on that march anyway," Andrew said.

"Then they'd never let me visit again," I pointed out.

"Yeah, I guess." Andrew began taking out some

games. "You're lucky not to have a family," he said.

"I do have one," I said, "in a way."

"Yeah, but not the real kind with everyone there," he said "That kind is a drag . . . You know where I'm going to live when I get older?"

"Where?"

Andrew always had said he was going to live on a very small island all by himself and just see people one half of the year. I was going to live on an island nearby and in the summer we would row back and forth and send food by a special pulley system. We would have our own animals and even learn their language.

"This cousin of mine came to visit." (Unlike Evelyn, Andrew has more relatives than you can imagine: four aunts, at least, and about sixteen cousins and even second cousins and great uncles. Once a year they all meet in a hotel, because otherwise they wouldn't all fit!) "He lives in a commune—you know, lots of people all together," Andrew said. "No one has to work, except at what they want. No one has to get married . . . Everyone does exactly what they feel like doing."

"But wouldn't it be noisy with so many people?" I said. It sounded like Mom's idea of children living all together.

Andrew thought for a minute. "You could bring ear plugs."

"There're always so many babies in those places," I said, "and they can stay up as late as they want."

Andrew doesn't like his baby sister, Colette, at all. He frowned. "Yeah, maybe the island would be better," he said.

Mom came by after supper. Andrew's parents were watching the T.V. news. Andrew's mother likes Mom, which is odd. She always hugs her and gives her things to eat, because she thinks she's much too thin. "Deborah darling!" she said. She says Deborah as though it were three words. "Abe, look, look at Deborah! She has these new shorts on."

Mom gave Andrew's father a kiss on each cheek. He likes her too. "There is no *filling* in these shorts," he said, gesturing with his hands.

"I'm getting fat," Mom said. "Look . . ." She puffed out her stomach.

Andrew said, "Everyone doesn't like being an *elephant*, Daddy."

Colette began throwing things out of her pen.

"So, does Brett like her new school?" Andrew's mother said. She had asked me all that already, but I guess she had to do it all over again.

"I guess . . . Don't you, Scratcher?"

Before I could finish, Andrew's mother said, "Andrew is devastated without his little Brett."

Andrew looked like he wanted to kill his mother.

"Such a lovely friendship they have," Andrew's mother said. "Such memories will be precious all his life."

Andrew was pretending to throw up in the waste basket.

Mom said, "So, listen, if Andrew does want to join us next weekend . . ."

There was this sort of long silence and then Andrew's father said, "It's true, I was a radical in my youth . . . One has to go through all this foolishness once, to get it out of one's system."

I thought Mom would really get mad at that, but she didn't. She just sort of smiled. "So, Andrew can come?"

Andrew's mother was looking sort of horrified, but Andrew's father said, "We'll see."

I looked at Andrew and we both were amazed because when Andrew's father even says, "I'll see," it means it really might happen.

On the way home Mom said, "Hey, Scratcher? Here's something you'll be interested in—Wednesday I have to cover a fashion show and Mimi's bringing a couple of her bassets."

Mimi is this friend of my mother's from college who trains the animals that they use in ads and on T.V. and stuff. Some of them have even been in musicals or operas, like if they need an elephant in "Aida." She lives in a great brownstone in the

Village and all the animals just go roaming around wherever they like.

"How come they need bassets for a fashion show?" I said.

"I don't know, something about 'dog-eared collars'." As you might have guessed, Mom is not exactly the most fashionable person in the world. But next to Mimi, she looks pretty good, though I really like Mimi. The only thing is, she likes animals so much, it's practically *all* she likes. She thinks *people* are funny. "So, want to come?"

"Sure . . . But how can I?"

"I'll write a note to school, saying you have to get out early for a dentist appointment."

That's one of the things I mean which is nice about living just with Mom. Children with fathers can never get out early from school, unless they really do have to go to the dentist. They must think I have terrible teeth at that school, because Mom never bothers to think up a better excuse.

Chapter Seven

How I Met
the Wolf Man

"Esmerelda, will you stop that, you fat head!" It
was Mimi, shoving one of the bassets.

The bassets—she'd brought three—were all girls.
They tend to look very droopy and old, but Mimi
says they look that way even when they're just
born. We were downstairs in what was sort of
like a boiler room. Upstairs was this kind of fancy
place like our school auditorium, only bigger. We
were supposed to wait downstairs till they called
up for the bassets. First there was going to be a
dress rehearsal, then the regular show. Mom said
they were showing spring clothes to women who

buy clothes for stores. If the buyers like them, they order some after the show.

Mimi handed Mom some chalk. "Go over Bessie, will you, Deb? I want her really white."

Mimi puts chalk over the bassets' white parts so they will really look clean. It's hard to make their neck clean, because there are so many folds. Also, the bassets keep sort of collapsing and rolling on their backs to be petted and then the chalk would rub off again.

"Listen, I've got to get upstairs," Mom said. She was going to take photos of some of the models in their dresses. "Want to come with me, Scratch?"

I shook my head.

"I have to go up, too . . . Wait a sec, Deb . . . Are you okay alone here, Brett?" Mimi said. "The dogs will be fine. Dry off Esme's jowls if she gets too drippy."

"Okay," I said.

The one thing I didn't like about being down in the boiler room was that it was sort of hot. Otherwise, it was kind of mysterious and interesting with no one but me and the bassets. If Evelyn was there, I knew she'd want to pretend we were imprisoned in a dark dungeon and the bassets were really princesses turned into bassets or something like that.

All of a sudden I heard some footsteps coming—

not from the direction where Mimi and Mom had disappeared, but the other side. It was a man with a very big dog, almost like a wolf.

"Are you part of the show?" he said.

"Not me, really . . . just them," I said, pointing to the bassets. They didn't look too happy to see the big dog and Clytemnestra began to growl. "You better not come too close," I said," or you'll make them nervous."

He laughed. "I thought bassets were never nervous," he said.

It was dark, and even from a distance, I thought he looked quite strange. He had bright red hair, not just gingery like Andrew's, and quite a large beard, even bigger than Andrew's father's. But aside from that, he didn't seem too scary.

"What kind of dog is that?" I said.

"She's an Irish wolfhound," he said.

"She looks like a wolf," I said.

"She's as strong as a wolf," he said.

He sat down about six yards away from me and the bassets settled down. "She's very gentle," he said. "You really don't have to worry."

"I'm not," I said. "They're not mine, anyway . . . They're Mimi's."

"Who's Mimi? Your sister?"

"No, she's my mother's friend from college," I said. It's funny, usually I feel shy with new people, especially grownups, but there was something odd about being in the boiler room and it made me feel quite relaxed. I told him how Mimi trained lots of animals.

"Mine is just a pet," he said. "I just do this some-times . . . if I have time."

"In our building we can't have pets," I said. "It's not allowed."

"That's terrible," he said.

"Well, in some ways; but Mom wouldn't have time to walk a dog if we did have one," I said, "so I'd have to do it and it might be too much bother."

"There has to be one person in the family who really likes dogs," he said. "In our family, it was my father."

"Well, I don't have one," I said, "so I don't know."

"Because they aren't allowed?" he said.

I laughed because that idea struck me as being funny. "No, they allow *fathers*," I said. "I mean dogs . . . I mean, it's a father I don't have . . . That's just because Mom didn't want to get married."

"I see," he said.

I wasn't sure he did, but at that moment Mimi came down and said, "How are my girls?" Seeing the man in the corner, she looked angry. Mimi doesn't like men so much, it's odd. "Could you please keep that dog away from here?" she said.

"Further away than six yards?" he said. He sounded angry, too.

"These dogs are quite nervous," she said.

"They don't look it," the man said.

In fact, the bassets were all curled up on top of each other, sleeping, their heads resting on each other's jowls. "Esme, Bessie, stand up!" Mimi said. "Do you want to come up with me, Brett?"

"Brett, that's a great name," the man said, laughing.

"When are you going on?" I said.

"Not till later." He waved as we all trudged up. "So long, Brett."

In some ways the man reminded me of this science teacher I had at my other school, but I'm not sure what it was. Partly the way he talked in this very regular way, as though he didn't know you were a child and he wasn't. Also, because of his beard, I guess. At first, they wanted Mr. Hensen to shave his beard, but then a lot of parents, including Mom, signed this paper saying he shouldn't have to and so he didn't.

The rest of the fashion show wasn't so interesting. Mimi and I watched from the sidelines as this model walked the bassets out down a ramp. They were very good and held their tails way up and Mimi seemed very pleased. I couldn't even see

Mom, but we met her afterward. Since we didn't stay for the end, I never saw the man with the Irish wolfhound. I was sorry about that.

Chapter Eight

Marching
in Washington

Andrew's father said he could come on the march in Washington. It was amazing in a way, but Andrew said sometimes his father just suddenly did things the opposite of what you'd expect.

We picked him up in Wally's car, since we were driving down with him and Nicky. Nicky, me and Andrew sat in the back and Mom sat up front with Wally. There was one very odd thing though: when Wally came to pick us up, he had a black eye.

"Did you have a fight?" I said. I'd really never seen a real black eye before.

"My wife did it," Wally said.

Mom was in the kitchen getting out some fruit for the trip. "You're kidding."

"Nope . . . she's taking judo, but that didn't work so well, so she decided to try this too."

"Did you give her one?" I said.

"Nope, I'm a non-violent type," Wally said.

I frowned. "But Wally, you mean she just hit you, even if you wouldn't hit back? That sounds so mean . . ."

"*I* thought so."

"Someone should hit her . . . That's terrible! you should've hit her back," I said.

"Of course he should!" said Mom. "Of course!"

Wally shrugged. "It's not my thing."

Mom believes in women knowing how to protect themselves, but I never saw her hit anyone. Her sister, Elaine, who lives in San Francisco, is a black belt in karate, though, and Mom thinks that's great. I might become a black belt when I'm older, but Elaine says you have to practice very hard and most people tend to give up.

I wondered why Wally's wife hit him if they weren't even living together anymore. Also, it seemed to me you wouldn't want to just hit someone if you knew they wouldn't even hit back. It would be sort of like stamping on a baby. I remembered what Nicky had said about Wally being like a baby.

"He doesn't know how to handle Rachel,"

Nicky said. (He calls his mother by her first name.) "She wouldn't hit me, boy!"

"Your mother sounds like a very mean person," I said. I really felt so sorry for Wally.

"She has problems," Nicky said.

"I never heard of just hitting someone like that."

"She says he provokes her by being so nice."

"That sounds mean too."

Nicky shrugged. It's funny, but he doesn't seem to care about stuff like that. I think if Mom ever punched someone, I'd feel terrible, especially if I liked that person, but Nicky is different. I guess you'd say he's cool.

Andrew and Nicky got along quite well. Andrew is much quieter—he never really acts up except at home, and he never talks back to grown-ups besides his parents. Also, he knows much more about things than Nicky. He had read all about the march in the newspaper and knew how many people were expected to come.

"I hope there won't be any violence," Wally said.

"There won't be," Mom said in that firm way she has.

I should mention that for the first time in ages Mom and I were both wearing dresses. This is a funny thing about Mom, but whenever we go on marches, she always has us wear dresses. And she wears this tweed coat which Grandma said she got when she was going to college, and she wears stockings and lipstick. That's because she says she doesn't want people to think the march is just a bunch of hippies.

"What's wrong with hippies?" Nicky said. He was in his usual raggedy looking orange T-shirt and jeans.

"Nothing," Mom said, "but for marches, you have to be straight."

I felt funny in the dress. I even had a barrette in my hair and patent leather shoes. The trouble is, there are so many people, no one notices what you wear. But Mom thinks it's important. She always says, "What if they interview us for T.V.?"

By the time we got to Washington, it was crowded. Luckily, it was not raining like last time. That was terrible, we got soaked and had colds for weeks. This time it was windy but nice. While the speeches were going on, Nicky and Andrew and I ran around. You couldn't hear much anyway, because the loudspeaker kept breaking down. Afterward, for the march part, Mom got us signs. I didn't especially care about carrying a sign, since it gets heavy, but Nicky wanted one. His said "Protest!" in big black letters.

"They won't know what it's protesting about," I said.

"They'll know," said Wally.

Mom had a big poster from her Women's Strike for Peace group, even though she wasn't marching with them. We were marching with a kind of anonymous group. We marched for about two hours and then I wished more than ever that I could've worn sneakers and not patent leather shoes. Toward the end, just as we were turning into this big field, I said, "Hey! There's the Irish wolfhound man!"

No one knew what I was talking about and they all stared at me. He was marching over on the other side, carrying a sign, too. I ran over to say hi. It was funny, I didn't really know him, but you never expect to meet anyone you've even seen before at these things.

"You're Brett, the basset girl," he said.

In the bright sunlight he looked even odder than he had in the boiler room. His hair looked even more bright red and he had funny skin, a little pitted, sort of. But what I liked were his eyes, which are blue and have this very kind expression. "We're all over here," I said. I brought him over and introduced him to everyone.

"Hey, your sign is better than mine," Nicky said.

"Take it," the man said.

"Hey, great!" Nicky took the sign even though

it seemed silly to me, since we were practically done marching. The Irish wolfhound man began talking to Wally and Mom. They were talking about how many people had come and stuff like that.

"I've been here since ten," the Irish wolfhound man said.

"We didn't get here till two," Mom said. "We missed most of the speeches."

"Hey Mom," I said. "Could we sit down, maybe, if you're just going to stand here talking? My feet hurt."

"Take off your shoes," Mom said.

I did and that felt better. Then we went someplace and Mom and Wally and the Irish wolfhound man had beer. Nicky drank some of Wally's beer—he likes it—but Andrew and I had ice cream sodas.

The Irish wolfhound man looked at Wally's black eye and said in a concerned sort of way, "Was there much violence? I didn't see any."

"Oh, his wife did that," I said. I said it right away, but when everyone looked at me, I thought maybe I shouldn't have. "She takes judo," I added, "but it didn't work so well."

The Irish wolfhound man didn't seem to think this was so odd. "My sister is a black belt in karate," he said.

"Hey, so is mine!" Mom said.

"You're kidding!"

"No, I swear."

"She *is*," I said. "She can throw a two hundred pound person over her shoulder and she only weighs a hundred pounds."

"I don't think I want to meet your sister," Wally said.

"No, Elaine's very sweet," Mom said. "She wouldn't hurt a fly."

"So's Susan," said the Irish wolfhound man, laughing.

"How come only women are black belts in karate?" Andrew wanted to know.

"They're not," the Irish wolfhound man said. "Most of them are men."

"It sounds sort of crazy, all these women throwing people around," Andrew said.

It's true, 'cause when you think of his mother doing it to his father, it does seem odd.

Then Wally and Mom and the Irish wolfhound man began talking about the speeches, so Andrew and I went to see what records they had on the jukebox. There weren't too many that we liked, but we put in our dimes anyway. Andrew plays the cello and likes all kinds of music, even rock, but I don't ever follow it that closely. I guess my mind wanders.

"Let us give you a lift back to New York," Wally said to the Irish wolfhound man.

"He won't fit," Nicky said.

"Sure he will," Wally said. "One of you can sit on his lap."

Of course, no one wanted to, because that seems so babyish. But we drew straws and then decided we all would do it part of the way. The good part was that the Irish wolfhound man seemed to know we hated it and didn't make any cute remarks to make it worse.

Chapter Nine

The
Yellow Submarine

The day after we got back from the march, I spoke to Grandpa on the phone for the first time. He was out of the Intensive Care ward and back in his regular room. Mom said he had already fixed it up nicely with his own paintings and hi fi set and everything. I wondered if he had any b,b, and c down there. Mom said that for the moment he couldn't eat at all, and he was all hooked up to different tubes and things till his insides got working in a regular way again.

"Hi, Mr. Jones," I said. "Your alligator misses you, you know."

"Misses me?" Grandpa said. His voice sounded

just about the same, maybe a little lower. "You know what that rascal has been up to?"

"No," I said. "I thought he was home in his tub."

"Home in his tub!" Grandpa said. "A likely story! That miserable creature actually snuck in here and now he's lying right under my bed and won't budge an inch. He's eating up all the nice food people send me. The nurses hate him, he's just a pest."

"Do they allow alligators in the hospital?" I said.

"Of course they don't," Grandpa said. "Someone might come and put him in jail any minute now."

"Did you tell him?"

"I told him, I told him. Do you think that did any good?"

"Goodness, Mr. Jones, I'm sorry to hear all this," I said. "You must be having quite a time."

"I am, I am," Grandpa sighed.

Mom said Grandpa was mad because the nurses come in to wake him up every half hour all through the night just to take his temperature. He put a big sign on the door, telling them to stay out, but they still wouldn't do it. Once he even threw a pillow at one of them, but it didn't help.

"I'd like to see Grandpa," I said to Mom after I hung up.

"You will, Scratch . . . after he comes home."

"When will that be?"

"When the doctor says he can."

It's funny. Even though I know our alligator stuff is just a game, in some ways I really imagine it's true, and it made me feel better to think of the alligator really being there in the hospital with Grandpa. I know that's silly, though.

That Sunday evening the Irish wolfhound man came over to watch movies when Wally showed them. His real name is Theodore, but I like to call him The Wolf Man because that sounds more interesting. Also, there was once this awful boy in my class at my other school called Theo, and I always think of him when I hear that name. Anyway, this Sunday Wally had "The Yellow Submarine," which The Wolf Man said he'd seen three times. That's the odd part about him—he seems to do certain things which you'd expect only children to do.

This time Mom sat down and watched most of the movie. Marshall wasn't there, just Nicky, so it was more of a grown-up gathering, which was good in some ways.

Wally didn't say much; he looked sad. Mom said that was because they think there might be something wrong with Marshall. They say he is slower than most children and they might have to send him to some special school. So many sad things seem to happen to Wally. Wanting to cheer him up, I went over and put my arms around him from the back and he smiled and almost blushed. "A creature from the feathery deep," he said.

The Wolf Man went inside with Mom at one point to look at some of her photos. She keeps the ones she likes best in some albums in the dining room. When she was gone, I told Wally, "I'm sorry to hear about Marshall."

In a way I wasn't sure I should have mentioned it, but I was glad I did. He said he felt very sad about it. I asked if they would be able to find a school for Marshall, and Wally said it wasn't so easy.

"At least he isn't wild or anything," I said. (Once I was friendly with this girl named Pamela whose brother had something wrong with him, and he used to do terribly wild things, like throw ink on the floor.)

"Ya, that's true," Wally said.

I heard Mom and Theo laughing in the next room.

"He has a dog as big as a wolf," I said to Nicky.

"Who?"

"*Him.*" I laughed. "I call him The Wolf Man, but don't tell him."

Nicky grinned. "He does look kind of shaggy like a wolf."

"He said his dog can really attack real wolves and kill them," I said.

"Doesn't do much good in New York," Nicky said.

"Can't tell," Wally said, "who you'll meet on a dark night."

"Oh, Dad, come on," Nicky said.

"The world is beset by dangers from within and without," Wally said. Sometimes he talks that way, especially when he's had too much beer to drink.

For a few seconds none of us said anything, and we heard The Wolf Man saying to Mom, "This one is worth the whole batch."

Wally smiled in a funny way.

Nicky said, "Hey, come on, let's watch the other half!"

"*I'm* ready," Wally said.

"Hey, Mom!" I yelled. "We're going to show the other half."

Mom looked in the door. "You go ahead . . . We'll be there in a sec."

Wally shrugged. "The lady says to start."

Nicky said, "Boy, I'm glad your friend Evelyn couldn't come tonight . . . Yuk!"

"I think Evelyn is a charming girl," Wally said.

Grown-ups usually find Evelyn to be charming.

"She has a lively imagination," I said.

Nicky guffawed. "Yeah, I'll say."

"Her main problem is that she wants to have a father," I said. "That's what she thinks about all the time."

"She's kind of crazy," Nicky said.

"What's crazy about that?" Wally said. "Most people want fathers."

"They do?" Nicky said this to tease Wally. I think it's kind of mean when he does that.

Wally started the movie, but actually Mom and The Wolf Man never came in at all. After it was over, they were still sitting in the dining room talking. Wally and Nicky had to go home and I had to go to sleep, so I don't know when he went home.

Chapter Ten

Making Bread

"I hear that Deborah is seeing someone," Grandma said to me when I went to her house that Thursday after school. Grandpa was still in the hospital but he was supposed to come home that Sunday.

When Grandma calls Mom "Deborah," I always forget who she means. I have this trouble with names. If I ever meet anyone with a certain name, I always think of that name with that person. And we once had a Deborah Calley as our music teacher at school. Even though we didn't call her Deborah, I tend to think of her as that, because the other music teacher, Mrs. Rugg, always said, "Now, Deborah, start playing!"

"The Wolf Man, you mean?" I said.

"Why do you call him that?" Grandma said.

Then I remembered that you can never use funny names like that with Grandma, because she always thinks they're real, and that he must really be a wolf or something bad. "Just for fun," I said quickly. "His real name is Theodore, but he has this Irish wolfhound."

"I'm so glad Deborah is seeing people again," Grandma said, pouring herself a cup of tea.

It's odd that Grandma should say that, because Mom always sees people. Isn't Wally a person? "Mom sees lots of people," I said.

"That's not what I mean," Grandma said, smiling.

All of a sudden I got a revolting idea: Grandma thinks Mom will marry The Wolf Man. Actually, Mom says if anyone even looks at her cross-eyed, Grandma thinks Mom is going to marry them. I think that's why Mom never tells her about things.

"Oh, she's not going to marry him," I said.

Grandma was silent.

It's funny. I don't see why Grandma wants Mom to get married so much. Neither does Grandpa. In fact, no one does. Grandma always says if I were a mother, I'd understand, but Mom is a mother and she doesn't understand. Mom says Grandma thinks everyone should be in couples like the animals going into the ark, but Mom says that's out of date.

"Mom is never going to get married," I said. "You know that, Grandma."

At that Grandma looked angry. "You don't know that for sure," she said.

"That's what she says," I said.

"Well, she says a lot of things," Grandma said.

"The Wolf Man bakes bread," I said.

"Is that how he makes his living?" said Grandma.

"No, it's his hobby. He has a lot of hobbies. He used to train dogs."

"But how does he live?" Grandma said.

"You mean earn money?" I said. That's another thing Mom and Grandma don't agree about. I guess Grandma thinks you need a lot of money and Mom doesn't, something of that sort. "He teaches in the evening," I said. "He teaches these special people who are behind in school, and never learned anything that well. He helps them catch up."

Grandma was stirring her tea. Suddenly she smiled in this sort of false way which was supposed to make me think that was all she wanted to know. She's really ashamed to ask Mom, because Mom will get mad at her, so she asks me, instead. I don't mind, only I think it's funny that Grandma is so ashamed. I wonder if Mom and me will be like that one day.

The reason I know about The Wolf Man making bread is this: one day I came home from school and Mom wasn't there. I let myself in and I heard this noise in the kitchen. Somehow I wasn't scared, even though I knew it wasn't Mom. It's odd, but some people make certain sounds and these sounds just didn't sound like Mom. Instead, it was The Wolf Man making bread. He was standing there punching this big pile of dough.

"Want to help?" he said.

He gave me a big glob of dough and I tried doing it. It was really great, and it had this very spongy feeling. I began punching it and tossing it around. He said you could do anything with it. Then we put it in a bowl and smeared butter on the top and let it rise.

"How come you make bread?" I said.

"I like it," he said. As I said before, basically he has an ugly face, because his skin is funny, but he has very nice eyes.

"Do you cook other things, too?" I said.

"Ya, I like cooking," he said.

"Mom doesn't, except for tartar steak," I said.

"I hear your Grandfather is feeling better," he said.

"Ya, I guess," I said. "I can't go to see him, because you have to be thirteen years old. I'll be twelve years old in two months."

"When I was twelve years old, my father died,"

he said, pulling at his beard.

I didn't exactly know what to say. I mean, if something happened so long ago, you don't know if the person still is feeling bad or not. "Was he nice?" I said. I wish I had said something better than that. Nicky always says "nice" is sort of a yukky word which people only use if they're too dumb to think of anything else.

The Wolf Man looked at me. He had a slightly sad expression on his face. He said, "It's hard to answer that . . . With me he could be nice, but he wasn't very nice to my mother. They didn't get along."

"That's too bad," I said.

"I missed him, though," he said. "Maybe if I had been older, we could have talked about things."

I said, "I don't mind not having a father because I can talk to my mother."

"That's lucky," he said. "Most people can't."

"She's sort of different," I said. "Some people think she's strange . . . Grandma thinks so."

"I think you're lucky," he said.

"Ya, so do I," I said. "This girl in our building, Evelyn, always says she wishes her mother would get married, but I don't wish that with Mom. Andrew says to have a regular family is a drag because then you have babies and act a certain way, and it's usually not nice for the older child."

The Wolf Man had been looking at me quite seriously, but then he gave a smile. "You may be right," he said. Then he went to uncover the dough which was all puffed up. Then he braided the dough so it would take on a certain shape. This is harder than you'd expect, since it's all gloppy.

"Will you leave the dough for us?" I said. "I mean the bread."

He said it was a present for Mom because she had gotten some prize for her work. It's funny that she didn't even tell me. Usually she does.

"That's thoughtful of you," I said. "Mom will like it. She likes to get presents, especially when it's not even her birthday or Christmas." I had to go in to do my homework, so I left him in the kitchen to do the baking part. When Mom came in later, he had gone home already.

And that's how I found out that he can bake bread.

Evelyn thought it was very strange. She came over after school and I showed her the bread.

"Men shouldn't do that," she said.

"Why not?" I said.

"If they do, they become like women and then there's no difference left."

"There's no difference anyway," I said. Actually, Mom says this and I'm not so sure, but with Evelyn you have to be extreme.

"Men who cook do other things, like dress up in women's clothes," Evelyn said.

"Well, Theodore doesn't," I said. I didn't call him The Wolf Man then, because I knew Evelyn would make up some big imaginative thing about it, and I didn't feel like hearing about *that*.

"My mother has a brother named Theodore who's crazy," Evelyn said.

"So?" I knew what Evelyn meant since, as I said, I have a thing about names, too.

"I'm just explaining my associations to the name Theodore," Evelyn said in a kind of snotty way.

There are times when you can take Evelyn and times when you can't. I said, "I like him, but you probably wouldn't."

"Why wouldn't I?" she said.

"Because he's ugly," I said.

Evelyn made a face. "Really horribly ugly, so you don't want to look at him?" she said.

"No, just ugly," I said. "But he has lovely eyes . . . Very kind."

"My mother would never have dates with an ugly man," she said.

If I had more courage, I would say certain words to Evelyn, like the ones Nicky uses, but I don't. I just said, "Evelyn, you know, you're a terrible conformist, you really are."

"Well, you're a terrible *non*conformist," she said.

"All good people are," I said. I don't know if I believe that either, but Evelyn makes me want to talk this way sometimes, the way Grandma makes Mom want to talk a certain way.

That night when Mom and I were having dessert, I said to her, "Evelyn is so dumb. She thinks just because Theo makes bread he must have something wrong with him."

"Oh, screw Evelyn!" Mom said. She uses language like that with me, but if she does it in front of Grandma, Grandma gets mad. Mom says that's hypocritical, since lots of grown-ups talk that way and there's nothing wrong with it. She says I can feel free to curse as much as I want, but the trouble is, once you know that, you don't feel much like doing it. I guess you partly have to think someone will get mad at you if you want it to be any fun.

"I don't mind that Theo is ugly," I said. "Looks aren't so important." I say Theo to Mom instead of The Wolf Man, because I don't know if she'd like that.

When I said that, Mom blushed, something she doesn't do very often. "Do you think he's ugly?" she said.

I felt awful. I had thought Mom must think he was ugly, too, but didn't mind. But after she blushed, I wasn't sure. "Oh, he just . . . has funny skin," I said.

"Ya," she agreed.

"Hey," I said, "two more days till I can see Grandpa."

Mom smiled. "Ya, it's happened so fast, hasn't it? Remember how we were talking about it happening?"

I was quite excited about seeing Grandpa again. We were going on Sunday. Grandma was driving down to pick him up very early in the morning and then bring him home. Then, later in the day, if he wasn't too tired, we would go over and see him.

Chapter Eleven

Sunday Morning

Sunday morning a funny thing happened. Usually I get up much earlier than Mom, as I've mentioned, and I just play in my room or do whatever I like. But this morning I slept a little later than usual, till nine, because I'd been watching this movie on T.V. till eleven or so the night before. When I was in the bathroom brushing my teeth, I heard this sort of thump in the hall, not like someone walking, but like something being dropped. I felt scared, more than I had the other afternoon. Maybe it was because I just couldn't imagine Mom being up that early. I suddenly began thinking that maybe someone had been hiding in the maid's bathroom in the back, next to the room where Mom does her developing and had just decided to come out. That bathroom always seemed to me the place where someone would hide, because it's so dark. Mom has these very heavy shades up for her developing and you can hardly see in there. I didn't know if I should go to see what it was—it might've been just something falling down because of the wind. Once, a picture fell off the wall, for instance, and fell on top of the water faucet and started it running. There was no reason for it, it just happened. Just as I was standing there, wondering what to do, I saw The Wolf Man come padding down the hall with the Sunday paper. He saw me and whispered "Hi!"

He was in his pajamas with a bathrobe on. I said, "Hi . . . You scared me."

"I'm sorry." He really did look sorry. "I dropped the paper."

I told him about the time the water had gone on all by itself and how I thought it might be someone hiding in the back room. "Is Mom up?" I said.

He shook his head. "Maybe we should start breakfast," he said.

This is one thing that is different about Mom and me. We don't have anything special for Sunday breakfast. Everybody I have ever visited has some special thing their mother always prepares just on Sundays, like pancakes or French toast. But Mom gets up so late, it's usually almost lunch time, and she mainly has coffee or something. So I just have cereal and eat it in my room. The Wolf Man wanted to make a real Sunday breakfast, though. Of course, men probably eat a lot for breakfast. Also, he might come from one of those families I've been talking about. He made bacon and French toast with heavy cream, which was very good. It was quite rich, but since I'm not too fat, I didn't care. I like rich things. Mom says that as a baby, I used to eat just the fat part off of ham.

We sat in the dining room and ate breakfast while Mom was sleeping. "How come you didn't sleep at your own house?" I said.

Mom hardly ever has friends sleep over, so that's why I asked. Like Mimi has never slept over. Mom always said she didn't want to have all the fuss of making breakfast for people.

"I thought it would be nice to have breakfast here," he said. He was acting a little funny. Usually, as I've said, The Wolf Man talks to me as though he were talking to a grown-up, but that time he didn't.

"Who will walk your dog?" I said.

"I have a neighbor who looks in sometimes," he said, "but I should go back later this morning.

Maybe after Deborah wakes up, we can all go over."

"Okay," I said. "Where do you live?"

This is really an odd coincidence. It turned out that he lives just around the block from where we used to live in the Village. "It's funny we never met you," I said.

"People never meet in New York," he said. He said he didn't like New York that much, because the air wasn't clean and stuff like that. People are always saying that about New York, but I never noticed it. I guess that's because I was born here.

Mom slept till twelve. Actually, we woke her up, because The Wolf Man said he was afraid she'd sleep all day. I told him how Mom says she really needs very little sleep and that she just sleeps a long time once in a while. Mom took a shower and got into a clean pair of blue jeans and a shirt and ate one piece of French toast. I could tell that she did it mostly to be polite, because she's usually not hungry in the morning. Then we all went over to walk The Wolf Man's dog.

His apartment was small—just one room, really, with not much in it. There was a table, a desk, a bed, and a kind of ruggish thing on the wall, and that was all. Norma, his dog, had a red mat near the window, which was quite nice. She seemed very glad to see Theo and began jumping up and down. I was a little scared of her because she was so big, but she didn't jump on us. I guess that was because we came with Theo, so she knew we were friends.

We took her to the park and let her go loose. She was very well-trained and always came when we called her, unlike this dachshund Mom and I once had, who never could learn anything. But our dachshund had lots of problems, too, like drinking all the time so he had to pee all the time. The only time he really ran was when he heard running water. Mom said there was something wrong with him and gave him back to Mimi. Mimi said there wasn't anything wrong with him, but he peed right in front of her, so you could tell there was something wrong.

"Will you come with us to Grandma and Grandpa's?" I asked Theo. I didn't want Mom to forget about that.

"Sure, why not?" he said.

I began wondering if Grandma would mind if he had a beard. She's not like that usually—sometimes she even says today's young people are lovely and stuff like that. It's hard to tell.

Grandpa looked tired when we saw him. He was in his pajamas. Grandma said he would start to work right away, since his office is right in their house. I went inside to play with Grandpa while

Mom stayed with Theo and Grandma in the kitchen. Grandma kept sort of staring at Theo in a way he might have thought was rude. I could tell Mom thought it was rude. Theo looked shy and pulled at his beard. I think he is a shy person. I'm not shy. People sometimes think I am because I don't always talk that much. But that's not the same as a shy person who wants to talk but feels funny about it. I know, because in my class at school there's this very shy girl named Susan Brownmotz, who always looks like she's going to die if she has to talk in class. Theo was probably like that when he was a child.

Grandpa sat in his reclining chair.

"How come you threw a pillow at that nurse?" I said, giggling.

"I should've done it sooner," Grandpa said. "That was my main trouble—those nurses. You know, nurses are supposed to be people who like to help you, but the ones there . . . Can you imagine this? Every half hour all through the night they came in to wake me up and take my blood pressure. My blood pressure's normal, but that didn't matter . . . Oh, never again!"

"Poor Mr. Jones," I said. But the idea of Grandpa throwing the pillow at the nurse struck me as funny and I started giggling again. "What did the nurse do when you threw the pillow at her?"

"She looked scared. I wanted her to think I was

crazy, so she'd be afraid to come near me again."

"Did it work?"

"Well, no one came in for the rest of the night." He grinned.

That's the thing with Grandpa. He does these crazy things that no one else would do. "Is that The Wolf Man?" he asked me. I had told Grandpa about my name for Theo.

"Ya, do you like him?" I said.

"He doesn't look very wolfish to me," he said.

"It's his dog, that is."

"Oh his dog! Well, that's a different story."

I knew Grandpa wouldn't care if Theo was ugly or if he earned lots of money or anything. He never cares about those things. I guess that's why Mom doesn't fight with him the way she does with Grandma.

"Mom must like him," I said, "because she let him sleep over at our house. He made French toast."

"Enterprising fellow."

"He's a very good cook," I said. I told Grandpa how Theo bakes bread and how Evelyn said that meant he must like to dress in women's clothes. Grandpa said that was silly, just like I thought he would, but I was glad to hear him say it anyway.

"You mustn't tire Grandpa out," Grandma said, looking in on us.

"She's not!" Grandpa yelled.

But, in fact, he did look a little tired.

Mom said, "Theo likes your African sculpture, Grandpa."

Theo sort of coughed and said something you couldn't hear so well. I felt sorry for him, being shy, even though he was a grown-up. But he never acts that way with me.

After we left Grandma and Grandpa's we went to an Italian restaurant to eat. That's my favorite, because then I can have ravioli. Mom always has veal with mushrooms. Theo had something with squid, which wasn't as bad as you might imagine.

When we got home (Theo had gone home by then), Mom put some music on the phonograph and lay down on her bed. "Do you think Grandma liked Theo?" I said.

She shrugged. "I don't know."

"Don't you care?" I said, surprised.

She smiled. "Ya, I guess I do. Do you like him?"

"Sure."

"Really?"

"Ya."

"Did you mind that he stayed over?"

I shook my head. "Andrew's father makes French toast on Sunday, too."

"Abe? How funny!"

"I think Norma is nicer than Archibald," I said, thinking of that dachshund we used to have.

"That's for sure," Mom said. She's always been sort of mad at Mimi because of Archibald. She claims that one reason we had to move from our old apartment was because Archibald peed so much over everything, and in the summer, especially, it had a terrible smell.

Chapter Twelve

Evelyn's Mother
and the Pills

That Monday a very strange thing happened. Usually I take the school bus in the morning, and I have to be downstairs at ten past eight. Evelyn's bus comes at eight thirty, but she usually meets me in the lobby at eight, so we can talk. She doesn't always do it, so I wasn't surprised when she wasn't there this time. But then, at about five past eight, she came down in her bathrobe. I should explain that Evelyn is just like her mother. She never goes slopping around in her bathrobe, not even when she's sick. Also, Evelyn's mother always gets up in the morning to make Evelyn breakfast. So when

Evelyn just walked right over to me in the lobby in her bathrobe and said: "Mom won't get up," it seemed very strange.

"Maybe she's sleepy," I said.

"No, she never sleeps late," Evelyn said, with this very worried look on her face. "She says she can't."

Evelyn looked so worried that I started to worry, too.

"Should I come up?" I said.

She nodded. I didn't exactly know what to do about the school bus, but I decided to have Pat, the doorman, say I would be in to school late. I could always go by regular bus. Evelyn didn't say one single thing in the elevator, which, for her, is quite unusual. Her face really looked white, the way they say people's faces look when they are really scared.

"Does she feel funny?" I said.

I had this pet rat once. When it died, its body felt cold. Of course, Evelyn's mother hadn't been sick and wasn't that old, so you wouldn't expect her to just die like that.

Evelyn's mother was lying sort of half out of the covers. When Evelyn went over and shook her, she didn't move, except to flop back and forth. "See what I mean?" Evelyn said.

Then I tried to shake her, but that didn't help

either. But at least she didn't feel cold. "Prick her with a pin," I said. "No, I know. let's throw a little bit of cold water on her face." We tried various things, like running an ice cube along her arm, but she still stayed asleep. Then we decided to go wake up Mom.

Even though Mom sleeps late sometimes, she always wakes up right away. Usually, I wouldn't have wanted Evelyn to see that Mom slept in her blue jeans, but I forgot to worry about that. Mom went with us right away to look at Evelyn's mother. Then she started making a lot of phone calls. She called the hospital and Evelyn's school and all sorts of things.

Then she said, "I'd like both of you girls to go to school right away."

That's not the sort of thing you'd expect Mom to say. I thought she would say we could do whatever we wanted.

"But I want to know what's happening!" Evelyn said. She looked angry, but also like she might cry.

"Darling, we won't know for at least a few hours," Mom said. "The hospital will tell us what's wrong."

Evelyn got dressed and the two of us left, but we decided not to go to school. Instead, we went to the fountain at Lincoln Center and sat there in the sun, talking. We agreed to go back at three, when we usually come home from school. Evelyn called the hospital once and pretended she was grandmother, but they wouldn't tell her anything. I guess they could tell she was a child.

It may seem odd, but that day turned out to be unusually nice. We went into the library and looked at books on ballet dancers. Evelyn once wanted to be a ballet dancer. She still takes lessons, but I think she's too short for that. Then we had lunch at a very nice place. It was sort of a cafeteria, where you could pick whatever you wanted. We thought of going to see a movie, but we were afraid it might get out too late, and we wanted to get home the same time we usually do from school. But, despite all this, we really were thinking about Evelyn's mother all the time. At least I was, and Evelyn must have been, because it was her mother.

I wondered what Evelyn would do if something happened to her mother. She doesn't have many relatives in America—only her grandmother in Texas, who has some sort of a sickness and her uncle, who is a bachelor. I don't think he would know how to look after a child. Of course, she always said she would like to go to Europe to be with her father. But she wanted to do that when she was older and could be his secretary and do stuff like that. It's too bad they don't let children live alone. Then Evelyn could stay in the same apartment and I could visit her and we could cook things together. But I don't think they would allow that.

When we got home, Evelyn went to her apartment and I went to ours. We just didn't want it to seem we'd been together, since we don't go to the same school. When I came in, Mom was on the phone, but then she hung up. She said that Evelyn's mother would be all right. Mom said that she probably got mixed up and took the wrong kind of pills before going to sleep. You know how some people have lots of different pills? Grandma and Grandpa do, because Grandpa is a doctor. Well, it seems Evelyn's mother had a lot, too. And since it was late at night and she was sleepy, she must have taken the wrong kind, or too many of one kind, and that was what made her so sleepy. But now she's okay.

I called Evelyn and told her to come over. When she did, I told her all about it. I had thought she would feel much better, and maybe she did, but when I had finished telling her, she burst into tears. Mom kept patting her on the shoulder and saying everything would be all right. Then she brought us cookies and said Evelyn would stay at our house till her mother got home.

That night Evelyn told me she thought her mother had taken the wrong kind of pill on purpose.

"How come?" I said. I knew what she meant because I once saw a movie about someone who did that.

"She was feeling quite sad," Evelyn said.

"What about?"

"That man John."

"The one I met?"

Evelyn nodded. "She thought she was going to marry him and then something happened."

I thought Evelyn must feel very badly about her mother feeling so sad she actually wanted to die. It made me sad, too, but in a funny way, it made Evelyn's mother seem more real instead of being so cheerful and well dressed all the time.

"He wasn't even that nice," Evelyn said.

I nodded.

I told Evelyn about how The Wolf Man had been there on Sunday when I woke up. I guess I wanted to tell her something from my life that was unusual or something like that. She said that if The Wolf Man had slept over at our house, it must mean that he and Mom had sexual intercourse. She said that was why grown-ups slept in one big bed instead of separately, the way children do. I had learned about sexual intercourse at school, of course.

I told Evelyn that Mom said people have sexual intercourse because they enjoy it. Evelyn said her mother said they do it to have babies.

"It might be something that doesn't sound good, but you would get used to," I said.

"I don't ever want to *try* it," Evelyn said, making a face. "I don't have to if I adopt a child."

"I don't want to adopt a child," I said.

"Why not?" said Evelyn.

"It might be funny in some way," I said, thinking of Marshall.

"Your own might be funny, too."

"But then it would be your own fault, in a way."

After we turned the lights out, I started wondering if Mom and The Wolf Man did have sexual intercourse like Evelyn said. It's sort of odd to imagine it.

Once Nicky showed me this book he found at Wally's house which showed couples doing it, but it just looked like people doing exercises. They were sort of smiling and looking embarrassed, maybe because they were having their picture taken.

Evelyn's mother came home from the hospital in much less time than Grandpa. She looked and acted just the same as usual. I think maybe Evelyn was wrong. Maybe her mother didn't want to die, and had just gotten mixed up with the pills. Mom said sometimes people feel both ways. They say they want to die, but really they don't. If they *really* wanted to die, probably they would. I can imagine what that's like, because once I felt so mad at Mom that I imagined what it would be like if I was dead and she felt sorry for being mean. Grandpa said lots of people think that way.

"I feel sorry for Evelyn's mother," I said to Mom. This was the first afternoon Evelyn wasn't there.

"Ya, I do, too . . . I never really did before," Mom said.

"Because she wears so much makeup?" I said.

"Not just that . . . her whole way of life."

I was going to tell Mom how Evelyn thought her mother had taken those pills because she was sad about that man John, but that reminded me of The Wolf Man. I asked Mom if she and The Wolf Man had sexual intercourse from sleeping in the same bed.

She said yes, they did.

"Will you have a baby, then?" I said.

She shook her head. Then she smiled. "Would you like me to?"

"No, you're too old."

She burst out laughing. "I'm only thirty-one."

I guess if you're a grown-up, it's different. But to me, thirty-one seems quite old. "You don't know anything about babies," I said.

"I had you."

"That was different." Maybe since I can't remember being a baby, I can't picture Mom doing all the things Andrew's mother does with Colette, like feeding her in a high chair.

"Grandma thinks you and Theo might get married," I said.

I expected Mom to laugh at that and say something mean about Grandma, but she didn't.

"Do you think I should?" she said.

I couldn't tell if she was serious. "No," I said. Then I went into my own room.

I really don't think Mom should get married. I don't think she would like it, because she isn't used to it. If you're married, you have to live a certain way. You have to do things at certain times. Also I guess I'm afraid Mom would be different if she was married. She would be more like Andrew's mother, and probably wouldn't take me places. She and The Wolf Man would do things together, and I would have to stay at home with some babysitter like Mrs. Wizen, which I would hate. Besides, they don't allow dogs in our building, so The Wolf Man would have to keep a special apartment just for Norma, and that would be expensive. There are lots of reasons against it and not that many for. But I think Mom knows that. She wouldn't just go and do it. She's not like that.

Chapter Thirteen

Trying not to Change

Grandma and Grandpa might have to move to Arizona. That's what Grandpa said when I went there on Thursday. He said the doctor thought the climate would be better for his health. I felt terrible when Grandpa told me. If he moves to Arizona, I will hardly ever see him.

"You can fly out on a plane," Grandpa said.

"I don't like planes," I said.

Arizona is all the way across on the map—I remember that from geography. Also, there aren't big buildings, mostly just dry places with lizards. I don't see why that would be so good for your health. Grandpa says it's because the air is very clean and dry.

"Mr. Jones, if you do that, where will your alligator go?" I said.

"He can stay here with you," Grandpa said.

"They don't let pets live in our building."

"Then he could come with me."

"On the plane?"

"Why not? He loves to fly."

"No, he doesn't, Mr. Jones," I said. "He hates to."

"He told *me* he loves it."

"Well, he told *me* he hates it."

At that moment Grandma looked in and said, "Brett, do you want to go to the store with me? I'm going to Andre's."

Andre's is this wonderful pastry store near Grandma and Grandpa's house. It has the most wonderful smell—much better than perfume. The nice part is that they give children free cookies. Sometimes this man (Andre, I guess) stands in front decorating a birthday cake, and you can watch him do it. He has this little bag, sort of like a tube, and he squeezes stuff out in different designs. He's so good at it and he never misses or makes a mistake. I want him to do my cake when I'm twelve.

I went to Andre's with Grandma. It was Mom's

birthday in a few days—she was going to be thirty-two, I think.

"That's pretty old to have a baby," I said.

Grandma got this strange expression on her face as though she felt sick. "Is Deborah going to have a baby?"

"No," I said. "Why?"

"Well, you said . . ."

"Oh, no." I laughed. It's funny that Grandma doesn't know about sexual intercourse. They probably didn't teach it at school when she was little. I told her about how Mom *could* have a baby but wouldn't. "She just has sexual intercourse because she enjoys it," I said.

Grandma kept looking around, still with this funny expression. There are some things you can't discuss with Grandma, because she's very nervous. Like when she found out about Evelyn's mother, she kept saying, "What a terrible shame! What a terrible shame!" even though Evelyn's mother was all right. I even told her that Evelyn didn't mind, because she knew her mother had been feeling sad and then Grandma just walked away very quickly. She didn't even believe the part about the pills. She said Evelyn's mother had just been very tired and that's the reason she hadn't been able to wake up.

Grandma is quite illogical about some things. Anyone knows you don't just not wake up because you're too sleepy.

"What kind of cake should we get?" Grandma said.

"Chocolate."

"All chocolate through and through?" Grandma said. (She thinks that's too rich.)

"Yes," I said. I knew that since it was Mom's birthday, Grandma would say yes.

The man named Andre wasn't there. But a lady behind the counter gave me three cookies. "She's lucky—she doesn't have to watch her weight," she said to Grandma.

Grandma smiled. This lady always says she thinks Grandma is my mother. I don't see why she thinks that, but Grandma smiles when she says it. "You have a nice, young Grandma," she says to me in this funny voice, like I was just four or five years old.

Andrew hates women like that. He came to our house that weekend. I told him how Grandma and Grandpa might move to Arizona. I didn't tell Evelyn because she doesn't see her Grandma and Grandpa that much and wouldn't know how sad that could make you feel. But Andrew understands, 'cause he even has two Grandpas.

"Hey, I have a great idea!" he said. "You could hide in their bags and go along."

"But who wants to live in Arizona?" I said. Andrew always thinks things like that are adventurous, but I don't. If you were packed in someone's bag, you might smother.

"It might be great," Andrew said. "You could have your own horse."

"I don't like horses," I said.

Anyway, I know Mom wouldn't like to go to Arizona. But when I said that to Andrew, he said, "So, you don't have to take her. You can leave her here."

"I would miss her," I said.

Andrew said I just thought I would. He said his cousin went away to prep school when he was thirteen and had a wonderful time. However, boys are probably different in that way. And maybe his cousin had parents that were very mean to him.

"I hate it when things change," I said.

"But they have to," Andrew said.

"Do you hate it?" I said.

Andrew said no, things had to change, and you wouldn't want to be a child all your life.

It's funny. People always say that, but I don't think it would be so bad to be a child all your life —not a *baby*, but a child of eleven or twelve. I wouldn't mind that. Maybe in a few years they'll invent a special drink or shot that will let you choose whatever age you want to be and then stay that way.

"What if you changed your mind?" Andrew said.

"Then you could change back."

Then Andrew and I tried writing a science fiction story about some people who changed to all different ages and then lost the stuff to put in the shot and couldn't change back. Some of them were stuck being small babies, and they got very mad.

Some people don't seem to mind changing, though. Evelyn, for instance, is looking forward to being an adolescent, so she can go on dates like her mother and go dancing and things like that. I don't know if I would like that so much. I hope being twelve takes a long time.

Chapter Fourteen

Mom Gets
in a Bad Mood

For the next month or so, The Wolf Man slept over on Saturday night almost all the time, and sometimes he came for dinner during the week. He likes tartar steak, too. Only he makes it a different way. He takes a whole onion and peels the outside part off. Then he just slices off pieces and eats them, the way you would with a loaf of bread. He says raw onion isn't really sharp, but sweet, if you get used to it.

Sometimes, when Mom had to work late, he would stay and babysit for me. He used to bring some papers to correct and sit in the dining room and mark them up. Sometimes he would tell me about his students. He said he thought I would like this Black girl named Martha, who was also interested in science. He said maybe someday we could go to this lab where his brother works. I bet Andrew would like to go, also.

One weekend Mom got into this terrible mood. First, she had this big argument with Wally on the phone. (I know it was Wally, because I answered the phone.) Usually Mom only argues with Grandma, at least in that yelling sort of way. But this time she was yelling and cursing, and even after she hung up, she stayed in a bad mood all day. I wished that I had someplace to visit, because when Mom is in that sort of mood, you don't want to be with her very much. Usually she just goes into her darkroom and develops pictures all day and hardly talks to anyone. Sometimes she lets me come in and watch her but not when she's in a mood like that.

I thought that Theo would come over that evening and that we might watch some movie on T.V. or something, but he didn't come. When I asked Mom why he didn't, she got very mad at me.

"Well, it's not *my* fault," I said, making a face at her.

I went in my room, but I felt mad. That meant Theo wouldn't be there that Sunday and we couldn't have French toast.

I got up early in the morning like I always do, and tried to make some French toast myself. It was fairly good, but not as good as when Theo makes it. I think that was because I used too much butter.

Then I had this idea. I decided to go down to see Theo myself. We could take a walk with Norma in the park, and it would be better than just mooching around the house all day with Mom in such a bad mood. Usually, I would have waited for Mom to wake up. But she says I can travel by myself in New York during the day, as long as I don't speak to strangers. Anyway, on Sunday there are always lots of people around, and you can take a bus down Fifth Avenue which lets you out right near Theo's house. I called Theo to see if he was there. I wasn't afraid of waking him up, because he gets up early like me. He said it was fine if I came down. I left Mom a note on the kitchen table, saying where I was. I left her one piece of French toast under this plastic hood so it would stay warm—only I knew she might not even eat it.

I enjoy going places by myself in New York, especially when it's something unexpected, like the day Evelyn and I didn't go to school because of her mother. I used to pretend I was running away, but lately I just pretend I'm grown-up and can do whatever I like. I passed Mimi's house while I was walking to Theo's place. I thought of visiting her, too, but then I remembered I had told Theo I would be right over. Maybe later, I decided, I would take Theo to Mimi's house and show him all of her animals. I don't remember if Mimi has an Irish wolfhound or not.

Theo's room, as I've said, is small, but he seems to be quite neat. An example of this is that he keeps his books stacked the right way in the bookshelf, and not upside down and on their sides like ours. He was sitting at his desk writing, and Norma was lying in the sun. Norma knows me now and doesn't growl or anything. But sometimes even though she's being friendly, she'll knock you down. I guess she doesn't realize how big she is, compared to an average person or child.

"I hope Mom doesn't mind, because I just left her a note," I said, sitting down next to Norma.

Theo looked a little worried at that. I guess he thought I had told Mom I was coming over. "I go places by myself all the time . . . I didn't want to wake her up, because she's in a very bad mood."

"I know," he said. He looked like he was going to say something, but all he said was that he had to correct some papers before we went out.

I got some books from his shelf and sat in the sun with Norma, reading them. Norma is a very good pillow. She doesn't mind if you lean back on her backside. I started some science fiction stories, since I thought I should find out more about them now that Andrew and I are becoming writers. But only one was really good.

When Theo was finished with his papers, he made himself some tea, which he makes from leaves in a box instead of a bag and drinks out of a glass. He gave me some milk. I told him about the story Andrew and I were writing. "I hate things to change," I said. "That was what gave me that idea. I'd like to continue being eleven. The trouble with being twelve is you become an adolescent and you get mad at everyone all the time."

In an absent-minded way, Theo said, "Eleven *is* a good age." Then he looked sort of worried again.

I asked him if he and Mom had a fight, and he said yes. I said I imagined it must be about getting married, because that's what people who aren't married wind up arguing about. He said that it was, in a sense.

You can't be sure of what people mean if they say "in a sense." I said, "You better not get married."

"Why not?" he said.

I drank a long swallow of milk. "Well, I don't think Mom is the type to get married," I said. "She wouldn't like it. Also, she might have a baby and she's too old for that."

"She wouldn't have to have a baby necessarily," Theo said.

"People usually do," I said. "You might not know that, since you've never been married. And Mom wouldn't remember what to do anymore, like with baby food. It was years ago when she did it with me. By now she's probably forgotten how, just like with math—she doesn't know the new math at all."

Theo frowned. "I wonder if *I* would be any good married."

"I don't think you would," I said. I had thought about this a lot, so I knew what to say. I was glad, because sometimes you forget the main things you want to say. "You don't know anything about children."

"Don't you think I could learn?" Theo said.

"I don't think so. Men usually can't, especially after a certain age." I didn't know how old Theo was. "After thirty-one, it's hard to learn those things," I said.

"I'm thirty-four," Theo said.

That meant he was even older than Mom! "Children make a lot of noise and it would get on your nerves, since you're not used to it," I said.

"You don't seem to make so much noise," he said.

"I do at times." I reached down to scratch

Norma's ears. "Anyway," I said, "there's another thing—your dog."

"What about her?"

"She couldn't live in our building, because they don't allow pets."

"We could move someplace else," Theo said. "We could move to Arizona."

"But that's where Grandma and Grandpa are going," I said.

"I know . . . that way we could live near them and you could still see them."

I made a face. "But all they have in Arizona is cactuses . . . You just go there if you're sick and need special air."

Theo said he was born near there, in Montana. He said it was beautiful country.

"I don't like horses," I said. "Their teeth are so big. Evelyn once had a horse step on her toe, and she said it was the worst thing that ever happened to her."

"You have to know how to handle them," Theo said.

"Anyway," I said. "Mom has her job and in Arizona all they have is ranches."

Theo laughed. "You're a real city girl," he said.

I turned red. I didn't know if he was making fun of me. "The main thing is," I said, "people who are married live a certain way . . . Mom would never like that."

"What way is that?" he said.

"Oh, married people always do things at certain times. They have to have dinner every night at six. The mothers have to wear dresses and Mom never does."

"Why couldn't three people just live together however they wanted?" Theo said.

"It just never happens," I said. I could tell Theo didn't know very much about being married.

It's funny, but I found it much easier telling Theo all those things than I would Mom. Maybe it's because I don't know him as well. Also, Theo doesn't seem like the type who would get mad at you. And he listens very carefully and doesn't say silly things or joke around. Only at the end he just began staring out the window with this funny expression. I was afraid that I had hurt his feelings.

"You could live with us and not be married," I said. At that Theo just said he thought we should go out and walk Norma.

We had a long walk in the park. It was a beautiful day, not too hot. I imagined Mom was just getting up, and was probably still in a very bad mood.

I took Theo to Mimi's house. She wasn't home, but her secretary, this man named Joseph, who helps her take care of the animals, was there. He made Norma sit in the back till the other animals got used to her. There was even a kangaroo named Wilhemina, that was very sweet. She was holding a cracker with these very small hands, and one of the bassets came around and snatched it away. Mimi has a lot of pictures of animals on the walls. There's one white cat that Mimi says earns fifty dollars an hour.

"Cats are usually very stupid," I told Theo, "but this one isn't."

I could tell that Theo really liked the place. He sat down and Joseph told him how one of the great danes had cancer.

"I didn't know dogs got that," I said.

"Yes, big dogs especially," Theo said. He and Joseph both like big dogs best. I think I would like a basset best, because they're funnier.

While we were sitting there, having lemonade, Mimi came back. She had this cat in a cage. She had taken him to some studio to pose for an ad with china. I don't think Mimi had seen Theo since that time at the fashion show.

"Where's Deb?" she said.

"She's home in a bad mood," I said.

Mimi laughed.

"Is it all right if I call her?"

"Sure." Mimi handed me the phone.

It took a long time for Mom to answer, but it

usually does. I told her about our walk and that we were both at Mimi's. She didn't sound quite so mad anymore. "Would you like to speak to Theo?" I said.

After I said it, I realized that Theo hadn't said he wanted to speak to Mom. But he got on and started talking. I didn't listen, because Mimi took me in to see a bird she had just gotten. She doesn't usually have birds, but this one was quite beautiful, all sorts of colors.

After we left Mimi's, Theo said he would come back home with me. I figured he had told Mom that he didn't want to get married and now she wasn't mad anymore. I was glad we had talked about that.

"Hi, gang," Mom said quite cheerfully when we came in. I could tell she wasn't mad anymore at all. She even said we should all go out for pizza, which we did, and we even went to a movie.

It was a very good day.

Chapter Fifteen

Things Change Anyway

A week or two later a horrible thing happened. I was sound asleep, when all of a sudden Mom woke me up. She didn't even click on the light, so I could at least see who it was. She said she and Theo were getting married.

I really felt horribly sick. I can't even describe it. At first, I thought she said they *had* gotten married, without even telling me. But to hear that they were going to do it anyway was more than I could believe. I couldn't believe Theo would do that after I had that long talk with him and told him how bad it would be.

"You'll have a father!" Mom said. She looked really excited and happy.

"I don't want one," I said.

"But you like Theo."

"So? Why does he have to be my father just because I like him?"

Mom looked away. "Things won't be different, Scratcher, I promise."

"You'll have babies."

"No, definitely not."

"But babies just happen."

"No, they don't. I promise not to have one unless we all decide it would be good."

I tried going back to sleep, but I couldn't for a long time. I thought how ironical it was. Evelyn would have been so happy to get a father—maybe *her* mother would like Theo! Here I had said I didn't want anything to change and *everything* was changing. Grandma and Grandpa were going to Arizona, I was going to be twelve, Mom was getting married, and I was going to have a father. If I had known being eleven would be like this, I certainly wouldn't have wished I could be eleven all my life.

"Gee, you're so lucky!" Evelyn said when I told her. She almost looked like she was going to cry.

"What's so lucky about it?" I said.

"Everything good happens to you," she said.

"You get everything."

I've learned that you can't argue with people when they're in a mood like that.

"How did he propose?" Evelyn wanted to know.

Evelyn is the type who probably imagines that people get down on their knees and say, "Will you marry me?" and that sort of thing.

"People don't propose anymore," I told her. "They just agree to do it."

"That's not very romantic," Evelyn said. "I would never do it that way. I would want something that I could remember later on."

Sometimes I think Evelyn will get married before her mother, because she thinks about all these things so much.

At school and everywhere I went, everyone kept saying how wonderful it was and how great I must feel. It doesn't matter what you say, people just keep thinking it's wonderful if that's what they want to think. So after a while, I stopped saying anything and just smiled in a phony kind of way.

The only person who understood was Andrew. When I told him, he said, "Gee, that's too bad, Brett," in just the right sort of voice. Maybe Andrew and I should go away to that island now, instead of waiting till we're older. It might not be a bad idea.

Grandma, of course, was happier than anyone. She didn't talk about anything else for weeks. Even Grandpa didn't seem to think it would be so bad. But, of course, he doesn't live with us, so what does he know?

Now we have to move again. For several Sundays I went with Theo and Mom to look at apartments. We have to move, because our place doesn't allow dogs, and Theo's place is too small. We looked a lot and finally found a place that has a very big terrace. Mom said she would put plants on it. They gave me the master bedroom. Mom and Theo said children need much more room because they have more stuff, like toys and things, and they spend more time at home. I thought that was considerate of them. Sometimes grown-ups surprise you like that by suddenly being considerate. I certainly do like the idea of the new room, which is around three times bigger than my old room. I could practically have a whole laboratory in one corner, or keep a white rabbit, or whatever I want. I can sleep out on the terrace in a tent in the summer. That part seems quite good.

Another good thing is that Mom swore that she and Theo won't have a baby. She said that if they do have one, they will adopt one and I can help pick it out. I've been thinking about that. I wonder if you can adopt a child of eleven. Then

I'd have someone to play with all the time. But I'd also have to share my room, and I don't know if I'd like that. Too bad we can't adopt Andrew. I think a boy would be better, because otherwise, it will just be Theo with all girls and he might feel funny, especially since he's never been married before. We might get an Indian. At least I can help pick it, which is better than having it happen suddenly, without knowing what's going on.

Mom said we will all visit Grandma and Grandpa in Arizona, and if we think it's very nice, we will move there. I do feel sad about Grandma and Grandpa leaving. Grandpa says he feels sad, too, but he knows his alligator will like it.

"I didn't know they had alligators in Arizona," I said.

"Of course they do," he said. "Haven't you heard of the famous alligator ranch out in Tucson? They have the finest, greenest alligators in the world! They live just on b, b, and c."

"I'd like to see that ranch," I said.

"You will when you come out to visit," Grandpa said. "You won't believe your eyes."

Theo says he will teach me to ride if we move out there, but I don't know about that. First I will have to see if I like it.

They decided to have the wedding at Mimi's. It was my idea, actually. That way even Norma could be there. Mom, of course, liked the idea very much. Grandma thought having all those animals around was strange, at first, but then she agreed. I guess she was afraid if she didn't agree, it might not happen. I went with Grandma to order the cake. We ordered it at Andre's. I told Andre to put a little dog and a girl on top, as well as a man and woman, and he said he would do his best. Actually, he did do it, except the dog didn't really look like Norma, it was more like a cocker spaniel.

The day before the wedding Mom suddenly began acting funny. By now I'd gotten used to the idea of the whole thing. I mean, if you can't do anything about it, it's silly to make a big fuss. But Mom said, "Oh, it's awful . . . giving in to convention like this. Why did I let the two of you convince me to go ahead with it?"

Us convince *her!*

"Mom, come on," I said. "Pull yourself together."

"I don't want to wear a white dress and all that crap," she said.

"So, don't," I said. "Who said you have to?"

"Grandma," she said.

"So, wear a white dress for the getting married part and then change," I suggested.

"Hey, Brett, you're a genius," Mom said. She

looked at Theo. "Isn't she?"

Theo had been looking at Mom like he knew the whole thing was silly. He winked at me. "Of course she's a genius," he said.

They said it was going to be a small wedding, but that I could invite some of my friends. So I invited Evelyn and Andrew. Nicky and Wally were coming, too.

The morning of the wedding I brought Mom and Theo breakfast in bed. They both looked sort of scared and nervous, and I even had to butter their toast. To tell the truth, I even had to eat most of the breakfast, which I shared with Norma. (We had smuggled her in for one night.)

"Thanks, darling," Mom said. I hoped she wasn't going to throw up. I read that people getting married do that sometimes.

I felt sorry for them. It must be worse if you're grown-up and not used to being married. Now they will have to be together all the time, even when I'm grown up and live on an island.

Mimi had fixed up her place pretty well. There were paper lanterns and things hanging from strings. The wedding part was supposed to be outside in the yard, where the dogs usually are, and Mimi had it all hosed down. The dogs looked very clean, like they had had special baths.

The man who was going to marry them was a

Unitarian minister named Parnell Wainscott. He looked nervous, too. I don't know why, it might have been just his expression. Evelyn was all dressed up, of course, even more so than me. She had on a white dress with a big pink sash. Her dress stuck out as though she had on a special petticoat underneath. Mom looked different, maybe because she was in a dress. She had her hair loose and looked younger. Everyone said she looked just like me.

We all stood in the yard while the minister read the vows. They were funny, sort of like poetry, except at the end they had to say "I do" and kiss and all that stuff. It was funny, because when they kissed, Norma began to growl. I guess she's still a little bit jealous. I gave her a piece of wedding cake so she'd feel better.

The cake was really good. Andrew and I ate it outside on the steps. Andrew even drank two glasses of champagne. I was afraid he would get drunk, but he said it just made him sleepy. I tasted it but it made my nose feel funny, as though I had to sneeze. Andrew gave Wilhelmina a piece of wedding cake and she ate it very delicately, holding it in her tiny hands. We decided on our island we will have a kangaroo, too.

Grandpa sat down most of the time and poured champagne and kept saying, "Let us drink to this good man." Mom laughed a lot and acted silly.

She kept taking photos of everyone and Grandpa said no one would know it was *her* wedding. (It was true. Of all the pictures she took, hundreds of them, there are hardly any of her. It looks like Theo was just getting married all by himself.)

"When are they going on their honeymoon?" Andrew asked.

"They're not going on one," I said. I told him how we were all going to Africa that summer instead, to see wild animals, like Mom and I had always planned. I was going to get a camera of my own.

"You've really got it made," Andrew said. "I wish my parents had gotten married now instead of before I was born. I didn't even get anything out of it."

"Where's Wally?" Theo said. "He was here just a minute ago."

"He went upstairs to lie down," Mimi said. "He's allergic to dogs and he had to take an antihistamine."

I decided to go upstairs and bring Wally some champagne and cake. I walked up the stairs. The upstairs part of Mimi's house is cool and smells nice. Wally was lying down on this wicker bed with his hand over his eyes.

"Wally?" I said. "Here."

I waited while he put his hand down. When he

saw me, he smiled. "Hey, kid!" he said. You look so grown up."

I smiled. I felt sorry for him in a way, being allergic and all that. But he did drink the champagne, which was just in a paper cup.

"So, a new life is beginning for you," Wally said, sneezing. "Here's to the new life!"

Walking downstairs again, I wondered if he was right.

About the Author

Norma Klein grew up on the East Side of New York's Manhattan. As a teenager, she traveled to France on the Experiment in International Living, across the United States on a bicycle trip, and to Russia for a Youth Festival. She attended Cornell and Barnard where she graduated cum laude with a degree in Russian, followed by a graduate degree from Columbia in Slavic languages.

One of the author's sixty published short stories appeared in *The Best American Short Stories of 1969*. Two others have received O. Henry Awards. *Love and Other Euphemisms*, a collection consisting of a novel and five short stories, has recently been published.

Norma Klein is married to Erwin Fleissner. They have two daughters, Jenny and Katie. This is Norma Klein's first book for young readers.